An award-winning author, Anne Cassidy has written over twenty books for teenagers. She is fascinated by the way ordinary people can be sucked into crime and forced to make agonizing moral decisions.

Praise for Anne Cassidy's books.

"Totally gripping" *Books for Keeps*

"Dark, chilling and clever . . . Anne Cassidy reminds me of Minette Walters or Ruth Rendell" CELIA REES

"Always compelling" *Telegraph*

"Compassionate and unflinching" *Guardian*, JAN MARK

Also by Anne Cassidy:

Birthday Blues
Looking for JJ
Love Letters
Missing Judy
The Story of my Life
Tough Love

anne cassidy

SCHOLASTIC

To Terry

First published in 1994 by Scholastic Children's Books
An imprint of Scholastic Ltd
Euston House, 24 Eversholt Street
London, NW1 1DB, UK
Registered office: Westfield Road, Southam, Warwickshire, CV47 0RA

This edition published by Scholastic Ltd, 2006

10 digit ISBN 0 439 95001 5
13 digit ISBN 978 0439 95001 5

British Library Cataloguing-in-Publication Data.
A CIP catalogue record for this book is available from the British Library

Printed by Nørhaven Paperback A/S, Denmark
Papers used by Scholastic Children's Books are made from wood grown in
sustainable forests.

1 3 5 7 9 10 8 6 4 2

www.scholastic.co.uk/zone

ONE

Maggie Kennedy wasn't superstitious but it made her shiver a little to think that she had probably been one of the last people to see Caroline Mitchell alive.

Not that anybody knew that the ten-year-old girl was actually dead, but she'd gone missing about three o'clock on the afternoon of the first day of the school summer holidays.

Maggie had walked past her and her big-mouthed pal, Amy Cullen, while they'd been playing on some toddler's tricycle, going up and down the incline on the drive that led into the flats.

"You'll get run over!" Maggie shouted tersely as Caroline Mitchell sped past her, down the step of the pavement and on to the road with a bump. Her knees had been ridiculously bent up so that her feet would sit on the tiny pedals and she gave a forced laugh that sounded like a machine gun. "at at at at at at at".

Maggie looked on disdainfully, her five extra years, and her 32-inch "A"-cup bra, dividing her off from these "infants" (as she and Bridget liked to call them). She hooked her finger under the wire round the bottom of the bra and pulled at it to stop it riding up; she opened her mouth to speak, but the other girl, Amy, stuck her middle finger up in the air and then looked over to her friend and gave a shriek. It was the sort of noise that suggested someone had just stuck a knife in between her ribs. Maggie wished somebody had, and in her head began to picture the scene when she heard "Aymeeeee!" coming from the innards of the flats. The girl looked resentfully towards a window in the three-storey, brick building, turned away and slouched off up the drive.

When Maggie turned to go, Caroline Mitchell had left the tricycle lying on its side. Its wheel was still rotating in midair and Maggie had an urge to right it and tuck it into the side of the pavement. She didn't, though, and as she walked off the ten-year-old girl was leaning up against the wall of one of the gardens and gazing on to the road.

It was the last time Maggie ever saw her.

It couldn't have been more than two or three minutes later that Maggie caught her first ever sight of a strange-looking man going into the house next to hers, a battered brown suitcase in one hand, and a black plastic bin liner full of something draped over his shoulder.

It wasn't just the fact that he looked odd that made her stop in her tracks, it was where he was going that surprised her. He was unhooking the gate of number fifty Coopers Road, a gate that had been closed for years, closed from long before she and her parents had moved into the adjoining house.

The most striking thing about him was the pronounced limp he appeared to have, as though he'd had a stroke or had lost the use of one of his legs. His face was thin and lined and his hair hung down to his jaw; he would have looked like a hippy only he was wearing an old-fashioned two-piece black suit. It was when he paused to open the front door that she noticed his earring, a gold hoop that glinted at his cheek.

The name "Long John Silver" jumped into her head.

The man looked round at her suddenly and opened his mouth as though he was going to say something. She jumped with embarrassment and, using both hands to pull each side of her bra down, she turned her head away from him and number fifty and went into her own house.

Passing the kitchen, Maggie saw her mum lying prostrate on the floor, her great pregnant stomach looming up out of her print dress, looking like a pouffe that someone might put their feet on.

"What's the matter?" Maggie said, not unduly alarmed. During the recent hot weather she had become used to finding her mum in all sorts of strange places and positions. A couple of days previously she'd been sitting on the edge of the bath with her feet submerged in cold water, a mug of tea resting in the soap tray. At eleven o'clock the night before she'd found her lying on a lounger in the back garden.

"Nothing. The lino's cool."

"Um. . ." It was all that extra flesh she was carrying around with her. Maggie had helped her mum get out of the bath that morning and hadn't been able to take her eyes off the lump; it was creamy and solid and looked like a giant bald head.

"Where have you been?" Her mum lifted her head up off the floor.

"I went to get some stamps but . . . you know . . . it was so hot, I couldn't be bothered to go all the way to Baker's Arms. I'll get them tomorrow. I've not even written my letter yet." She said these things out loud to her mum but really she was talking to herself.

"Quick, she's moving!"

In seconds Maggie was kneeling beside her mum. She put the palm of her hand on to her mum's stomach and held it still. After what seemed like a long time, she felt a gentle pushing movement against it, three or four times.

"She's kicking," Maggie said, even though what she'd felt was nothing like a kick; rather it was a slight nudge, probably the baby's shoulder rather than its knee or its elbow.

"She's a big girl now!" her mum said, squeezing Maggie's arm.

"Thirty-four weeks!" Maggie said. She'd counted. She'd started on the Tuesday her mum had told her she was pregnant. Seven weeks then. Now it was thirty-four. Six weeks to go.

They sat there for a moment, in the middle of the kitchen floor, two smiling faces. Then Maggie said, "Shall I get you a cold drink?"

"Would you?"

"For you, fatty, anything."

Later, on her way upstairs to get her mum's book, she said, "It looks like someone's moved in next door. . ."

"What?" her mum shouted, but Maggie was already in her parents' bedroom, looking around for the current tatty paperback that her mum was wading through. She opened and closed the dressing-table drawer and looked idly out of the window to see if Caroline and Amy were hanging around again. She heard the sound of next door's front door banging.

It was a sound that she wasn't used to and she couldn't resist pulling aside the net curtain and glancing out. The odd-looking man went out of the gate and got into an old black car that she hadn't noticed before.

There was no sign of Amy or Caroline.

They were probably annoying someone, somewhere.

She shook her head and continued to look for the book.

It was nine o'clock when she finally sat curled up in her chair and started to write to Bridget.

Dear Bridget, she began,

Now it's only five weeks and four days until you come back from Waterford.

She stopped, her pen in midair.

She could ask her about the plane journey; that was only going to take one line, though. She could tell her about the new man moving in next door; except there wasn't really a lot to say about him. She could give her the latest update on her mum's condition; she was heavily pregnant, but then Bridget already knew that.

Maggie let the pen rest on the arm of the chair and the writing pad slip sideways on her lap. She couldn't think straight. She was tired. She'd finish it tomorrow. She let her head lie back against the soft fabric of the chair when a commotion from downstairs made her lift it up again. She could hear her mum's voice crying and her dad shouting to someone from the front door. It sounded as though there were a number of people outside the house.

Her mum was going to have the baby, she was sure.

She dropped the pad and pen and ran out of her room. Her mum was sitting on the bottom stair, half crying, half taking to Mrs Rogers from three doors down, who was standing with her bedroom slippers on in the doorway.

"What's the matter?" Maggie said.

Her dad was putting his shoes on and there were a couple of men outside the door clicking torches on and shining them on to the pathway and then turning them off again.

"What's happening? Is it Mum? Is the baby coming?" Maggie said.

In the distance Maggie could hear the "nah nah, nah, nah" of a siren, and in her head she pictured an ambulance tearing along the streets coming to pick her mum up and take her off to hospital.

"Mum, shall I get your case?" Maggie said, a note of fear in her voice. They'd gone through the emergency procedure a number of times but she still felt afraid.

"You stay with Mum," her dad said. "I'm off to join the

search." The siren had come deafeningly close and then abruptly stopped. Through the door and across the way Maggie could see a police car parked in the middle of the street, not an ambulance.

"What search?"

There was a bustle as her dad and the neighbours left and jostled with each other down the front path. The front door slammed shut and Maggie sat down on the bottom stair next to her mum.

"Are you all right?" she said, not knowing what was happening, where her dad had gone.

"It's not me," her mum said, grabbing her hand and holding it tightly for a moment. "It's little Caroline Mitchell. She's not been seen since this afternoon. Her poor mother's been looking for her since five o'clock. Now that Cullen boy from the flats says he saw her get into a man's car this afternoon."

Maggie sat back. Caroline Mitchell was missing. She saw her for a moment, balancing on the tricycle, her knees resting on the handlebars, a smirk on her face.

"He's just back from football, see. It was about four o'clock that he saw her." Her mum blew her nose loudly into some kitchen roll. "She got into someone's car," she said, shaking her head from side to side. "The little fool got into someone's car!"

TWO

"We searched everywhere. If that girl was within a mile of these streets we'd have found her." Maggie's dad was still in his pyjamas, even though it was nine thirty.

"Won't you be late for work?" Maggie said, unsure as to how she should respond to this information about Caroline Mitchell.

Her dad was about to speak when she heard her mum's voice: "Your dad was up until the early hours. He can go in to work late."

Her dad closed his mouth and nodded in agreement.

"Where did you look?" Maggie said.

"We looked in the open spaces first. The small parks and bits of greenery." Her dad was drinking a giant mug of coffee and her mum joined in.

"Like that triangle of bushes over by the shops at the bus garage."

"And the adventure playground round the back of the primary school."

"And the tiny playground over the back of the high road."

"But how could she be there?" Maggie said. "She'd be obvious, wouldn't she? Anyone passing would have seen her."

"We weren't. . ." her dad started.

"They weren't just looking for a . . . for Caroline herself. They were looking for things of hers or bits of her clothing."

Maggie's mum took a deep breath. Her face had the expression of someone who had just inhaled a nasty smell.

"When we didn't find anything, we started on empty gardens, disused shops or factories, lock-up garages. There was a crowd of us. We split up into groups with different police officers. One group did one set of streets, the other group. . .

"Your dad was looking around the Park Estate, the flats."

"She could be anywhere, you see. We had to unlock garages, walk up and down the stairs of the tower blocks. . ."

"Sixteen storeys."

Maggie found herself looking from her mum to her dad, waiting for the next comment. It was like a tennis match, only no one was scoring points.

"The worst bit was looking in the giant bins. We couldn't just glance in the top. The policeman told us of cases where the . . . child . . . had fallen in and been buried deep in rubbish for hours or even days before she was found."

Maggie's mum had her arms protectively around her lump.

"They were up and down this street all night," her mother said. "They went into the gardens of people who were on holiday and knocked up everyone else. They even went into next door's garden. I saw them walking down to the sheds at the bottom with the new man."

"I didn't hear anything." Maggie had tried to stay up late but had ended up nodding off on the sofa about midnight.

Her mum's face brightened for a moment. "Tell her about the lorry," she said, smiling across to her husband.

Maggie tensed herself, waiting for the story.

"There was this smallish refrigerated lorry parked in the flats' car park. The police found out the name of the company and the address of the employee. We had to wake the bloke up; two thirty it was by then. He only says. . ."

"He came to the door in his underpants, your dad said," her mum continued, as though her dad had just been called away and was unable to finish his own story. "And when he saw the policeman at the door he put his hands up in the air, as if they had a gun, and said, 'It wasn't my idea to take them. It wasn't my idea. You ask the foreman.'"

"We said," her dad came back, reclaiming his old ground, "We said, 'We need to search your lorry,' and he said, 'See the foreman, see the foreman. I was only doing what he said.' He kept his hands up in the air as though we were all standing with revolvers aimed at his chest!"

"They get to the lorry." Maggie's mum had let go of her stomach and was using her hands to mime someone slowly turning the great handle of a door. "They open it. And inside, what do they find?"

Maggie paused, any foreboding she had had dissolved. The story wasn't serious; the glee with which her mum and dad were telling it told her that.

"A dozen packets of smoked salmon. Your dad found them behind some empty boxes."

"Bloody cold it was."

"And the man is confessing all the time about how these smoked salmon were a part of a load that was going to Harrods and how they wouldn't miss it and how he and the foreman were going to take them to a local restaurant."

Her mum and dad were smiling at each other.

In her head Maggie imagined the steaming sides of the refrigerated truck, her dad stepping carefully up the middle, directing the beam of his torch into corners. behind boxes, not looking for smoked salmon. Looking for a little girl with a loud mouth.

"But no Caroline," she said. 'You didn't find Caroline." She looked at each of her parents in turn.

Her dad stopped smiling and picked up his newspaper. "No we didn't find Caroline," he said. He looked uneasy, as if someone had just told him off.

Her mum stood up and started to move the dishes off the table to the sink. "Your dad says if she doesn't turn up by tomorrow they're going to drag the Hollow Ponds."

"And would you say that Caroline was happy or sad when you last spoke to her?" The policewoman had her pencil poised, ready to write on her pad.

Maggie screwed her face up. How could she answer that? Caroline was as irritating as she usually was whenever she saw her.

"Happy, I suppose," Maggie said, thinking of her dreadful laugh: "atatatat".

"And would you say that Caroline had plans to go anywhere, or do anything unusual when you last spoke to her?"

Maggie was sitting on the wall of the flats. There were small knots of people standing about on the pavement. A few feet away Maggie could see Amy Cullen and her mother talking to another policewoman. John Cullen was sitting further along the wall.

There were a couple of men from the local newspaper, one of whom had an expensive-looking camera hanging around his neck.

"I don't think so," Maggie said looking across to the cameraman. What if she got her picture in the paper? She was one of the last people to see Caroline alive, after all. That would certainly be something to send to Bridget.

"No, I don't think she was going anywhere." She wasn't being much help. The woman was asking such difficult questions. Why didn't she ask her about things that she knew about; things about Caroline Mitchell and how annoying she could be. She let her eyes slide to the side and looked at John Cullen. He was staring at his feet. She looked down along the pavement and saw that he had unfashionable trainers on. She shook her head at his lack of taste. If Bridget were here she'd have something sharp to say.

"Did you, or have you noticed any special car driving around the area in the last few days? Perhaps one that you haven't seen before, or one that seemed to be just cruising around?"

Maggie had noticed about two thousand cars driving round the area in the last couple of days. How was she supposed to remember any particular one of them?

"No," she said noting, with some annoyance, the newspaper people sidling up to Amy Cullen and her mum.

Another police car turned into the street and cruised slowly towards them. A flutter of anticipation went through the small groups of people and the cameraman turned towards it.

"Another car."

"They might have news."

"Maybe they've found her."

"It's the mother."

"If you think of anything at all, please contact us down at the station." The WPC was folding her notebook away and walking towards the newly arrived car.

Maggie stood up and found herself joined by Mrs Rogers, still in her bedroom slippers.

The crowd moved together as the car door opened. The camera flashed two or three times, before the WPC stepped in and said in a loud voice, "I've told you people to keep back. I won't tell you again."

A frail-looking woman got out of the car. Her face was pale and her hair was standing on end. Maggie hardly recognized her as the same woman she had seen week in, week out, walking behind or in front of Caroline; calling her in for her tea, remonstrating with her on the street.

She looked unsteady on her feet and the WPC put her arm out for her to lean on. The crowd was perfectly quiet for a few seconds. Then a small mumble grew and Maggie heard Mrs Rogers' voice in her ear.

"Last time I saw her with a woman police officer she was being led out of Sainsbury's for shoplifting."

Maggie closed her eyes with distaste. What a bitch! The best thing to do was to ignore the woman. Caroline's mother walked into the flats. The photographer was squatting precariously on a nearby wall, his camera and zoom lens jutting out from his face, making him look every bit like some bizarre oversized bird that was waiting to pounce.

The quiet murmur rose again as people began to review the latest developments.

"She's aged ten years in one night."

"She looked like she was on drugs to me."

"They give them tranquillizers, I've heard."

"They'll be looking for her old man, I suppose."

"No one's seen him for years. . ."

John Cullen was still sitting down, oblivious, it seemed, to anything that was going on. Possibly he was thinking of the last time he saw Caroline. Maggie pursed her lips and walked off.

When she got to her gate she saw that the newspaper man had walked over and sat down beside John Cullen. A second or so later she watched as the photographer swooped down off his perch and landed on the wall beside them.

It didn't look as though she was going to be in the newspaper after all.

THREE

It was five whole days since she'd posted her letter and there was still no reply.

It had been short; she'd told Bridget about Caroline's disappearance and about the new man next door. She'd had plans to write a lot of details describing the events but when it came down to it she hadn't known how to start. In the end she'd written about six lines. Looking at it had reminded her of her English work at school. The words "could do better" jumped into her head.

It deserved an answer, though; five days was a long time.

Maggie stood at her mother's bedroom window and watched the postman as he drifted in and out of gateways, whistling gently to himself. She narrowed her eyes with irritation as he passed her door and ambled across the street and up towards the flats. He stopped abruptly for a moment and her face relaxed: he'd found a letter for her mixed in with the others; he wasn't used to delivering letters to Ms M. Kennedy; he was coming back and she'd soon be curled up in her favourite chair reading Bridget's letter. But the postman pushed against the rotten gate of number fifty, and she felt cross again and craned her neck to see if the strange man opened his door to get what she thought should have been her letter. The angle was impossible, though, and all she saw was the postman's smiling face and she heard him shouting something about not being used to calling there and then the gate closed behind him and he was on his way again to the flats.

She couldn't work out why Bridget hadn't replied.

It was nine thirty and there was no point in going up to the Hollow Ponds until about midday.

She sighed and walked out into the hall and into her own bedroom.

She could hear the sound of the hoover from downstairs and the bumps of furniture being moved around. She rolled her eyes. Her dad had told her mum to stop all the heavy housework. A couple of mornings ago he'd actually shouted at her and Maggie had seen her mum's eyes glaze over and her dad cuddling her and stretching his arms to reach right around the lump.

Her mum had taken no notice though.

The previous day, after her dad left for work, Maggie saw her red-faced in the middle of cleaning cupboards and polishing the back windows.

About ten thirty she had crumpled on to the settee.

"Don't tell your dad, now promise," her mother had said, puffing and sucking in breaths. "He doesn't understand."

Maggie had made her a cup of tea and brought her the newspaper. From then on her mum spent the day between bursts of frenzied activity and periods of seeming collapse. After lunch she'd gone out in the car (even though her dad had insisted that she wasn't to, had said that her size made it dangerous to drive) and went to Walthamstow market for a walk up and down the stalls. A couple of hours later she'd struggled out of the car carrying bags of fruit.

Maggie had filled up a basin and placed each of her mum's feet gently into lukewarm water. She'd got a towel and patted each foot until it was dry.

"Now have a rest," Maggie had said. "You've got to take care. Rest, rest and more rest was what the book said."

"Whose side are you on? Dad's?" her mum said, a mock frown on her face. "Listen. We women have got to stick together."

That's how it had always been. Maggie and Mum against Dad in cards; Maggie and Mum arguing for women's rights when Dad got lazy and tried to get out of ironing his own shirts; Dad and his temper trying to put together a self-assembly wardrobe while Maggie and her mum were in the other room, their hands clamped over their mouths to stop the laughter exploding out.

Late in the afternoon her mother had a shower and then sat reading her book. When her dad came in he bent over to kiss her and said, "You look rested love."

Later he looked at the glittering windows and the tidy cupboards and hugged Maggie. He gave her a couple of pound coins and said, "Don't think I don't know what you do."

There was no point in owning up, no point at all. It would only start rows between her mum and dad. Maggie put the coins in a tin box in her drawer, together with the others he'd given her over the past weeks. She resolved to buy something for the new baby with them. Now and then she emptied them out on to her bed: five she counted, then six, then eight. She spaced them out on her duvet so that they made a giant "M".

Over the last couple of days, fed up as she was without Bridget, she'd imagined herself taking them to Selbourne Walk Shopping Centre and seeing whether she could get a T-shirt or a CD or a poster to put in her bedroom.

After a while, though, she'd made a little tower with them on her bedside cabinet and they'd sat there until she swept them off with her hand and they'd clattered back into the tin.

Next time Dad offers me one, she thought, I'll say no. I'll just say no.

Maggie handed her mum a cup of tea.

"I don't want you going near the ponds. I don't want you around there when they're dredging that water. You haven't already been there, have you? Not after what I said?" Her mum was looking straight at her.

"No," she lied.

Maggie hated lying to her mum. Usually, if there was a disagreement, she would reason, persuade, or negotiate. In the end she would face an argument rather than lie and be found out afterwards.

In the last few months, though, her mum's condition had made that kind of discussion almost impossible. Instead of bantering and making arguments, her mum invariably raised her voice until it started to crack and then, within seconds, tears the shape of small peardrops hung on the corners of her eyes.

It became easier to avoid the argument and lie.

Maggie had been up to the ponds three times in fact.

On the first day it had been exciting. The woodland area was dotted with groups of kids on bikes, some cycling in everlasting circles, some standing in groups looking bored. There were knots of adults with prams and dogs, and what seemed like dozens of policemen trying to fix strings of white tape from bush to bush. A man dressed in diving gear had waded into the nearest, biggest pond; every ten minutes or so he reappeared, his steps splayed outwards, as though he had his flippers on the wrong feet. When he stood by the side of the pond and peeled his hood off there was a collective gasp from the small crowd as though they'd expected some totally different creature to be revealed. As he stood sipping a steaming cup of something an excited murmur fluttered around. Had he found anything? Was there any sign of her? Was there anything else in the muddy water?

They hadn't found anything, though, and the previous day Maggie had been one of the few people still standing watching. The three policemen who were there at the end had packed up and guffawed with laughter at something as they'd passed her. She'd stood for a while afterwards, watching a cow rakishly chewing, and thought about Caroline Mitchell. She'd looked hard into the brown water for a few moments and wanted to say, "Do you think she's there? All this, and she's probably not even in there," and roll her eyes exaggeratedly. But there was no one to say it to.

If only Bridget had put up more of a fight about going on holiday.

Maggie looked at her mum stretched out on the settee.

"Did you see that story in the paper about that woman who was told that she could never have children and then got pregnant?" A change of subject was needed. Maggie didn't want her mum to ask any more questions about the ponds or to think about Caroline Mitchell.

"Um?" her mum said, sipping her tea.

"She was thirty-eight when it happened," Maggie added. Her mum loved stories in the newspapers or magazines about older women having unexpected babies. "I'll get it for you."

A few minutes later Maggie left her reading quietly on the settee.

Getting off the bus at Whipps Cross, Maggie noticed a panda car with its headlights on overtaking the long queue of cars that was inching away from the roundabout.

In the distance, she could see a small crowd of people and kids on bikes around the boating shed. She could hear the sirens of two police cars cutting across each other, like a pair of distressed toddlers. Had they found something? Had they found Caroline Mitchell's body?

Maggie quickened her pace. She felt her breath shortening and when she was almost there she heard a voice from behind her.

"Hello."

She looked round and saw John Cullen riding towards her on his bike. He was on his own. There was no Amy. She continued walking.

"Hello," she said. He got off his bike and began to wheel it along beside her.

"They've found something. About ten minutes ago. The frogman came out with a black plastic bag."

About ten minutes ago and she'd missed it! She'd waited hours over the last few days and she'd missed it.

"What? A body?" she said, and in her head she saw Caroline Mitchell's face.

They reached the small crowd and Maggie saw a couple of women from the flats. They were mostly people that her mum didn't associate with; that her mum had said were "common". In the middle of them Amy Cullen stood, her hand perched on her hip, her voice cutting in and around the chatter.

"They've found something, you mark my words," one of the women said, leaning on a pushchair.

"I'll bet it's some remains," Amy's voice sang out.

"No, he didn't say a body, he said 'evidence'. I heard him say 'evidence'," said a woman who was sucking on an orange lolly.

"They never put them in in one piece. . ." Maggie could hear Amy's voice again.

There were two policemen with their backs to the pond, facing the small crowd: the frogman and some others were looking at something on the ground some fifty or so yards away.

"Nobody knows what it is," John Cullen said quietly. "It's just a black plastic bag. It could be nothing more than some old rubbish someone's thrown in." It was the longest thing he'd ever said to her. Usually his sister came thundering in with her opinions or her wisecracks.

Maggie looked at him. He had a nice face. She hooked her middle finger under the bottom of her bra and pulled it down. It was her turn to speak and she couldn't think of anything to say. She opened her mouth but words were jammed up somewhere down in her throat.

She heard Amy's voice from behind: "John. Over here!" As he walked away she couldn't resist looking down at his shoes. If only he didn't wear those particular trainers.

The policemen started to move towards the crowd and the frogman was placing the rubbish bag into another see-through plastic bag.

"What is it?"

"Is it Caroline?"

"Is it a bit of a body?"

"What about the rest?"

The policemen just ignored the questions and said, "Move along now. Move along." A small van that had come with the frogman moved on to the grass and towards where the plastic bag was.

"We can't make any comment about what we've found. It's police business. Now move along please."

John Cullen was back beside her. "My mate's mum works in the bread shop next to the police station. She'll know soon. I'm going down there. I'll tell you if I find anything out." Maggie pulled her gaze away from the departing van, the stern-looking policeman and saw John cycling off in the direction of the high street. She looked back to see his sister, Amy, remonstrating with the policeman, her hands on her hips.

"I was her best friend. I've got a right to know."

"She's got a right," the woman with the lolly chipped in. "Her mum asked me to be here. As her . . . her representative."

"Move along now." The policeman's face was impassive.

"Her representative," the woman with the lolly said.

It was typical that Amy would still want to be the centre of attention. Maggie shook her head and was about to walk away when her eye caught a familiar face over by the boating shed.

She was about to say "Hello" when she realized that she shouldn't be there. She looked away quickly and stood for a few moments, stricken with indecision. Should she tell her mum she was just passing? She got a phone call from the police to come up? She went for a walk and just ended up at the ponds? None of it would be believed.

Curiosity made her turn round to look again. The face was familiar but she couldn't immediately place it. The man wasn't looking directly at her but out towards the pond. His hair was long and stringy and his face looked pinched and worried. It wasn't one of her dad's workmates or any of the male teachers at her school. She turned back towards the crowd, which was waning now.

"It's a bloody police state!" She could hear Amy's voice.

Perhaps she had been mistaken and the man wasn't someone she knew; maybe he was someone on the telly. Maggie looked back again but there was no one there. Her eyes scanned the small crowd but he was nowhere. He had gone. She looked at her watch and decided to go home.

On her way to the bus stop she passed Amy Cullen standing beside a police van.

"Go on. Give us a lift. You'll have to go down and tell her mum any road. I could be there. I know her. It's just next to where I live." She grinned at Maggie.

Maggie turned her head away to avoid looking at her. It was then that she saw the man again.

He was walking along on the other side of the road and it was his limp that made her look twice. His hair was blowing back in the breeze and she could see his earring.

It was the man from next door, her new neighbour, and he seemed to be in a hurry, taking a long step and then rapidly pulling his other leg behind him.

Maggie looked to see if there was a bus coming that he might be racing for but there was not. She remembered then the old black car that sat outside his house.

A few seconds later he turned into a side road and Maggie lost sight of him. She shrugged her shoulders and walked on towards the bus stop.

A few minutes later she was joined by Amy Cullen.

FOUR

Maggie had forgotten all about the man next door until she heard her mum and dad talking about him that evening.

She was sitting on a chair in the front room with the headphones on. For a while she'd been listening to music and idly gazing across at them on the settee, her shoulders moving imperceptibly to the different beats.

Her dad had the newspaper spread out on the coffee table and was using one hand to turn the pages. His other hand was resting on her mum's stomach.

Mum was gazing into space. She had a restful expression on her face and Maggie saw her move one of her hands to cover her dad's hand.

Maggie rolled her eyes to herself. Since the pregnancy there were times when her mum and dad acted like young lovers. They frequently held hands or hugged each other while she was there. Once or twice she'd made a joke about it or told them to "grow up" but they'd just laughed.

Her dad, with a confident smile, had said that it was to do with his mature good looks and his attractiveness to women. Maggie's mum had winked at her at this point; Maggie knew that it was the pregnancy.

She looked over at the clock; it was five forty. If Bridget hadn't been in Ireland she'd probably be on her way to call for her.

She reached her hand over and turned the volume of the music up as loud as it would go without her mum hearing. Instead of trickling into her ears, the music seemed to come in a great wave that filled her head, crashing from ear to ear, the drums beating on the back of her neck, the piano rippling across her shoulders, the singer just behind her eyes and the back-ups above her sinuses somewhere.

If she had been on her own in the front room she would have loved to stand up and move around in the small area that the flex of the earphones allowed. She would make a fist with her right hand as though she were grasping a microphone and move it close to her mouth when the words of the song needed it. She would dance around like singers did at gigs she'd seen on the telly and make dramatic gestures as though she were acting out the meaning of the song. She would join in and sing out loud, closing her eyes for effect and reaching a hand out to an imaginary audience.

She knew she could always go up to her room and play it on her own stereo. Her mum and dad might even like to be on their own. The truth was, though, she was fed up with being alone up there; fed up with looking at four walls and making plans to pass the time until Bridget returned.

Every now and then the music stopped and in the silence the songs seemed to buzz and echo in her ear until the next one started.

It was between songs that she heard her parents talking

about something other than the new baby. She had watched their mouths open and close in a kind of silent movie where the music was out of sync with the action. When the song ended it was as though someone had suddenly turned their volume up.

". . . Ten years it's been empty. He's got a big job on his hands if he thinks he can renovate it. . ."

". . . And money too. It must have cost him something. . ."

The tape came to an end and she wound it back.

"He bought it years ago. He just never moved in, that's what I've heard."

"Who says? Mrs Rogers, I suppose. . ."

". . . She remembers, she said. About ten years ago. The old boy who lived there sold it to a family. He moved out and everybody expected the new owner to move in but no one came."

Maggie pressed play again. They were talking about the man next door. She pictured him hurrying along the road in front of her, dragging his bad leg behind him. The name "Long John Silver" jumped into her head again.

She knew if she turned round and joined in the conversation it would change, or at least bits of it would be censored. Then she'd have to wait until her mum was on her own to find out what they were talking about. She reached over and turned the volume down low so that she could hear what they were saying. She closed her eyes as though she was totally immersed in the music. The man's face came into the darkness behind her eyelids, as he had been, standing by the tree up at the ponds.

"But ten years in a mental hospital. It's not right, them putting him out just like that. And next door too. Nobody asked us."

"It's not our choice. He owns the house after all."

"Ten years. It's not right We should have been asked. Who knows what his background is."

"What do you want? The poor man to stay in a hospital for the rest of his life? You don't want that."

"And where's his family?"

"Perhaps he's divorced. Who knows? He just probably wants to be left alone." Her dad's voice was quiet, as though he was talking to a difficult child.

"I suppose so." Her mum didn't sound convinced.

"I saw him moving a lot of compost and a new mower in the other day. Looks like he's going to try and tidy up the garden. That should please you."

"Um. . . Mrs Rogers says that's what he does. Gardens, I mean. He gave her a little card with his name and phone number on."

"There you are. Nothing sinister in that. Maybe he could do our garden." Her dad sounded triumphant, as if he had just won a complicated argument.

The doorbell rang and they stopped talking. Maggie took the earphones off and sprang up with an almost automatic reaction.

"I'll get it," she said, but on her way out of the front room it came to her that it wouldn't be Bridget waiting for her on the step.

Her steps slowed as she got to the door. Before she opened it, she noticed an envelope on the floor. She bent down to pick it up and then opened the front door with her other hand.

There was no one there. She stepped out and looked up and down but she couldn't see anyone who looked as though they'd just come from her house.

Over the road, leaning against the wall of the flats, was John Cullen. For some reason she felt embarrassed and closed the door quickly.

"Who is it?" her mum shouted.

"No one," she said, tearing open the envelope.

Inside was a carefully written note.

It weren't a body they found. It was some old clothes and stuff. Nothing to do with Caroline. Amy wants me to go down to Lousy Park tomorrow and see if there's any sign of her. Come if you like.
John X

Come if you like. What a cheek! Maggie stuffed the note in her pocket and, using both hands, pulled the sides of her bra down.

"Who was it?" Her mum's head appeared at the front room door.

"No one," Maggie said.

"Those wretched kids playing about again!" her mum said, walking down the hall towards the kitchen.

* * *

It was 3.26 a.m. on Maggie's bedside clock. She heard the flush of the toilet and the click of the toilet door as it closed. She heard the sound of her mum's slippers as they padded across the landing.

Then there was silence.

She turned over in bed and closed her eyelids tight but in seconds they eased open again and she was left staring at the blacks and greys of her room. She looked at the clock. It was 3.29 a.m.

She began to think of the note that John Cullen had sent her and of the kiss that he had put at the bottom. Come if you like, it had said, and then John X. She tried to picture his face as he had been leaning up against the wall across the road and to see if it triggered any feelings inside her. She pictured him walking alongside her on his bike that afternoon up by the ponds to see if she felt any warm glow or sharp stab.

She remembered the racing feeling in her chest some months before when she and Bridget had started to take notice of the boys from the sixth-form college who used to hang around the same shops as they did at lunch times. She had spent ages in the girls' toilets at the beginning of lunch time, combing her hair and checking her eye make-up. She had felt a rising excitement as she and Bridget walked down the thin streets that led to the high road and almost had to take a deep breath as she turned the corner where the chip shop and the bakery were. She revised her habit of buying a large greasy bag of chips that was sprayed in ketchup and often left red marks at the corners of her mouth. Instead she bought a thin cheese sandwich that came in a see-through plastic triangle and took small bites from it, wiping her mouth with a tissue while she was chewing.

There seemed to be dozens of boys who hung around the three or four shops on the high road. Some were passing through, en route to the pub, some were buying cigarettes in the sweet shop, some were buying food. There was no particular boy that she or Bridget had focused on: there were leather jackets, smart haircuts; there were impassive faces chewing gum or taking mouthfuls from a can of Coke; there was a hand shielding off the wind while the other held a match to a cigarette. There was an earring, there was a smile and white teeth, there were throaty voices. There was no one boy. When she walked back to school with Bridget, gulping down the remains of her sandwich, she had in her head an amalgam of the boys she had been among. And for the afternoon she sat at her desk and let the feelings that this image provoked stab and jostle inside her chest.

She thought of the note again. It was the first time a boy had ever made an advance on her. She thought of John Cullen and the way he had talked to her up at the Hollow Ponds. There were no sparks of delight in her chest. Maybe John Cullen would always be just a boy from school who wore chain-store trainers.

In the middle of these thoughts she became aware of a nagging noise at the back of her head. She sat up and turned her bedside lamp on.

There was silence.

Then she heard the noise again. It was the sound of someone crying. She was sure it was her mother and she got out of bed and opened her door a crack to see what was happening. She listened hard but the noise seemed to have got lower, further away, and she looked across to the side window and realized that it was coming from outside the house.

The crying continued as she reached over and turned the lamp off. It was a sobbing sound, deep and throaty. She stepped across to the curtain and pulled it aside. Her window was open and overlooked the back of number fifty. The back door was wide open and a fan of light spilled into the overgrown garden. There was the sound of a nose being blown and sniffs and in her mind a vague picture of a child was forming. Children cried like that, long and solidly, forcing tears until there was nothing left, continuing the sobs even when their voices were dry and their throats relaxed.

Caroline Mitchell's face came into her mind, her eyes puffed and glassy. She had fallen from one of the factory windows in Lousy Park a year or so before and her sobs had gone on for ten or fifteen minutes until everyone told her to shut up or else.

She waited for a few seconds and watched the dark garden and the cone of light at the door. The crying stopped for a moment and then seemed to start again with force.

There was no child next door; only the new man, Long

John Silver, lived there. A picture of Caroline's face came into her mind again. The crying was loud for a child, even one with a mouth the size of Caroline's. It couldn't be a child's.

Maggie shook her head as though someone was there beside her and she was communicating her feelings. Inside her there was a growing unease. The crying continued and she saw the tip of a shadow in the lighted part of the garden. Excitement started to bubble in her chest. It couldn't be Caroline but if it were *she* would be the one that had found her. *She* would be the heroine. In a split second she saw herself being congratulated by the police, her mother's and father's arms around her, the flash of the reporters' cameras and the woolly microphones of the TV companies; in the corner somewhere Caroline's mum sitting, her daughter on her knee.

She found herself moving from one foot to the other, her back and arms tense with anticipation. She was on the brink of turning round and going for her mum and dad when she saw the man from next door walking out of the doorway, through the orange light into the dark of the garden.

The crying sound moved with him.

Maggie slumped against the curtain. It wasn't Caroline Mitchell at all. It was him.

A grown man, with long hair and an earring. A man who owned a house and drove a car, crying like a child.

She watched him for a few minutes wandering amid the gloom of his garden until the noise faded and eventually stopped. She closed the curtain and sat down on her bed, and amid the initial disappointment she felt a mounting sense of sadness that was vaguely linked with Caroline Mitchell and the man's ringing cries.

Pulling the corners of her duvet around her, she lay down and after a while went to sleep.

FIVE

Maggie slept till past ten the next morning. When she went down to the kitchen there was a letter on the table for her. She could hear her mum's voice from the garden and while she was making herself a cup of tea she watched her, leaning on the fence, talking to the man next door, Long John Silver.

She got a couple of biscuits from the tin and sat down to read the letter. It was two pages full of details about Bridget's holiday. The nice stewardesses on the plane; the long train ride to Waterford; her aunts' farm and the vicious geese; her cousin Brendan and his friends.

Maggie put the letter down as her mum came in from the garden, her face flushed from her exertions. She was smiling.

"Eddie's going to landscape next door. He says he's going to dig up the bottom and put a pond in."

"Eddie who?" Maggie said, looking resentfully at Bridget's letter. It was a wonder she had time to write to her at all with so much going on.

"Eddie, the new chap next door. He's a gardener," her mum said, going out of the room. Maggie heard the sound of her feet as she went upstairs.

A gardener. Maggie put the letter down and suddenly remembered him crying the night before. Up until then it had gone out of her mind, as though it had never happened. He'd been crying bitterly just a few hours before; then, once daylight came, he was leaning on a garden fence, discussing ornamental ponds with her mum as though nothing had happened!

And he'd been in a mental hospital for ten years.

Folding Bridget's letter and finishing her tea she heard the front door bang and a few seconds later her dad came into the room.

"There's a couple of your friends outside, Maggie. They asked if you were up yet."

It had to be John Cullen and his sister Amy. She wouldn't be able to get away with just not going. She'd have to go out and tell them. She huffed loudly.

"Me and your mum are going to be out for a few hours," her dad said not noticing and looking at his watch. "We've got an appointment up at Whipps Cross this morning and then we thought we'd go to Wood Green and look at some nursery furniture."

It meant she was going to be on her own for most of the day.

"You can get yourself some lunch, can't you, love?" he said, pushing a pound coin across the table at her. She picked it up without a word.

Her mother came in on a cloud of talcum powder. "Are we ready then?" she said, her face glowing. She had a dress on that was just too small for her condition and her lump seemed to be straining through it. Maggie thought she could even see the outline of her belly button. If

Bridget had been there she would have nudged her and they would have laughed.

Bridget wasn't there, though, and with the prospect of spending most of the day alone Maggie went up to her parents' bedroom window and looked down at John and Amy Cullen

A few minutes later, with her pound coin in her pocket, she found herself walking towards the high road with Amy on one side, giggling at one of her own jokes, and her brother, John, his unfashionable trainers standing out like snowshoes, walking a few feet behind.

They reached Lousy Park about twelve. They each had a bag of chips and headed for the old signal box behind Wilson's Veneers, a one-time wood-processing factory that had long since shut down.

They crossed the rusty railway lines to the side of the factory and rounded the one remaining truck that was slowly crumbling on to the sleepers. Giant weeds grew up between the flooring and a pale green creeper had locked on to the wheels.

Maggie tiptoed between the rails. Even though there had been no power in them for five or six years, she still made a point of not touching them. You can never be too careful, she thought.

It was a bit of a scramble to get on to the roof of the signal box but John Cullen held the girls' chips while they climbed, and then he passed the bags up to Maggie while he clambered up.

The three of them sat silently side by side and ate their chips. Maggie looked at the huge industrial park in front, all of it now disused. To their right was Wilson's, the last of the factories to be shut down. Maggie remembered the first time she had ever sat on that roof. She'd been in between her mum and dad and some other people. They'd been looking down on hundreds of people protesting at the closure of the factory.

The factory had shut down anyway and the estate, once known as Lordsley Estate, was rechristened "Lousy Estate". She and Bridget often came over on a Sunday for a bit of peace and a look at other groups of older teenagers who used it for unspecified purposes. There were always kids around too. They used the dozens of empty buildings to play in. Even though their parents had warned them to stay away from the area they still came in their threes or fours, making dens of empty outbuildings, playing by the river, finding treasure among the bits of unused metal. Once the police had visited all the schools in the area, telling kids to keep away because of an attack on a young boy along the towpath by the river. The following day it had been even more crowded than usual. Kids, teenagers, groups of older boys walking around with cans of lager, making loud hooting noises and trying to push each other into the river. She and Bridget had kept out of it and sat up on the signal box. They'd shaken their heads at such immaturity.

Eating her chips, Maggie looked at the great peeling sign that stretched across the side of the Wilson's factory,

"Veneer of the week – Sandalwood".

"Our dad was manager there." Amy said out of the blue. Maggie looked at her.

"He had a top job," Amy said, tightly screwing up her empty chip bag. "They gave him an office and a car." And with an overarm swing she flung the packet into the air. It landed a few feet away.

Maggie tutted and looked at John Cullen, who was staring across the empty park. There was no need to just chuck litter anywhere.

"He got killed in a motorbike accident. A head-on collision with a bus full of army cadets." Amy had a small packet of cigarettes open on her lap. She was counting them out on her knee.

"That's a shame," Maggie said, looking across to the far corner of the park, where the river touched the back of one of the factories. There were a couple of old tramps making themselves comfortable by a wall.

That was why Maggie had never seen Mr Cullen. He was dead. She looked to the side at John whose face hadn't registered anything that Amy had just said. Perhaps that was why he was so quiet; losing his dad had made him a bit peculiar.

Maggie heard a sudden shriek. She looked around, convinced that Amy had fallen off the side of the signal hut.

But Amy was grinning at her. "You believed me!" she said, and out of her mouth came a silent gasping laugh. "She believed me!" she said eventually, directing her comments to the thin air.

Maggie pursed her lips. She'd been caught again by Amy's big tales. How many times had she and Bridget rolled their eyes when they'd heard Amy talking about all the drugs she'd taken and the boys she was going out with?

She'd been off guard; she'd not thought that Amy would use parents as part of one of her lies.

"Very funny. Very funny," Maggie said. It occurred to her, though, that she had never seen Mr Cullen. "Where is your dad anyroad?" she said, folding her empty chip bag up in a small square.

"He works away," Amy said, the laughter gone from her voice. "On the oil rigs. He's a diver. That's why he's away from home a lot."

"Oh yes?" Maggie said, nodding her head with mock agreement.

"Really," Amy said.

Maggie looked at John, who was still eating his chips, slowly, with deliberation, as though each one had a different taste.

"Yes, all right, he's a diver and my dad's a film director," Maggie said.

"Please yourself," Amy said, moving from side to side on her bottom and rolling over on to her stomach to slide down the wall of the signal box. "Please yourself. Are we looking for Caroline or not?"

Maggie followed her down. There was no point in looking for Caroline here. The police would have searched this area first. It was a well-known play area for local kids.

John was beside her. "I'll take the east side, Amy, you take the west. Maggie you look through the centre buildings."

"What for?" Maggie said, feeling uneasy. "The police have searched here already. And if there is anything –" Maggie wasn't quite sure what she meant by "anything" – "then I don't want to find it on my own."

Amy looked at John and let out an overloud sigh.

"You and Amy go together," John said, "I'll do the buildings above Wilson's. You do the buildings that edge on to the river."

"Well we won't find anything," Maggie said, walking a few paces behind Amy, taking care, as she crossed the dead railway lines, not to come into contact with any metal.

About an hour later they got back to the signal box to see John already there. He was standing on the ground fiddling with something on the end of a stick.

"Find anything?" he said and continued to play around with whatever it was on the floor.

"Nah," Amy said. Maggie and Amy had walked around shouting Caroline's name out loud, kicking open the doors of old buildings with their feet. They passed three or four groups of kids, startled by the sounds they were making. Towards the end Amy picked up a rusty old length of metal and began smashing the one or two windows that were still intact. Maggie had looked guiltily around and kept saying "Ssh. . ." but Amy took no notice.

"Look what I found," John Cullen said, a smile on his face. He held the stick in the air like a fishing rod. On the end of it was a small balloon. Maggie looked closer until Amy let one of her shrieks out.

"Give us it here," she said, and John handed her the stick.

It was a condom. A pale pink see-through balloon that had lost its shape. Amy jerked the stick towards John and he jumped back out of the way, laughing. Then she thrust it towards Maggie. Maggie took three steps backwards and found herself within an inch of the railway line.

"Pack it in," she said, but Amy liked the game and began jumping towards her and John, first one, then the other. At first Maggie was cross but as Amy began to lunge towards her, like a swordsman in an old film, it became fun.

"Quick, round here," John Cullen said and Maggie followed him into the alleys between the factories. Amy, shouting gleeful abuse, followed close behind, holding the condom on a stick like a wand.

"Hide here," John said breathlessly.

Maggie stood in front of him in a small alcove, her heart galloping. "Ssh. . ." she said needlessly. She could hear Amy's voice around the comer. She felt John Cullen's arm slip around her waist. Amy, about to turn into the alley that they were in, changed her mind and began to walk away, towards an old set of sheds in the far corner. Maggie felt John's arm grip her tighter and didn't know what to say, didn't know whether she liked it or not.

Without a word though his arm dropped and he walked away from her, his steps gaining pace until he was almost running.

"Amy!" he shouted towards his sister, who had almost reached the buildings she was heading for. "Amy!"

Amy stopped and looked round and began to walk towards them. Maggie had almost caught up with John by then and noticed that his face had hardened and he was agitated. When Amy got close enough to push the stick at him, he grabbed hold of it and broke it in half and threw the pieces to either side. The condom flew off into the air and Maggie watched it float down to the ground like a deflated parachute.

"What's the matter with you?" Amy said with rage. "You didn't have to do that!"

"It was a stupid game. You can get diseases from them."

"It was mine anyway," Amy said. She had evidently forgotten that it was John who had found it first.

"It was stupid!"

"Sod you lot," Amy said and turned heel. Maggie watched her go, confused as to what had happened. John Cullen turned back to her and said, "Stupid cow," and, putting his hands in his pockets, walked off in the direction of the river.

Maggie was left standing in the middle of Lousy Park by herself.

"Charming," she said and walked off in the direction that Amy had gone.

SIX

Maggie lay back on the deckchair and let the sun burn into her skin. Out of the corner of her eye she could see her mum sitting on the lounger, a strapless sundress covering the lump, her face, shoulders and legs glistening as though someone had just rubbed her from head to foot with a knob of butter. On the ground beside her was a bottle of suntan oil.

On the ground beside Maggie were Bridget's last letter and the free newspaper. Bridget's letter was long and detailed, mainly about some boy cousin she had met and fallen for. She hadn't referred to any of the stuff that Maggie had written in her letter. All she had said was that Maggie could have written more. Their letter-writing was getting more and more like an English assignment. The next thing would be Bridget correcting her spelling and grammar.

The newspaper was full of the usual adverts and items about stabbings and fatal car accidents. The only thing of interest was a tiny column on the first inside page headed, NO TRACE OF MISSING CAROLINE.

It was two and a half weeks now and no one had seen or heard of her. Maggie wondered whether she really was dead. And if she was dead, why.

For the first time in years Maggie suddenly thought

about the Material Man. She looked across to her mum and was about to tell her that she had thought of him but stopped herself. Even though it was five years ago, her mum still got upset about it, still cried sometimes.

The Material Man. Maggie closed her eyes and visualized him sitting behind the counter in his shop, his small glasses glinting under the bare light bulb that hung above, his button waistcoat making him look like a bizarre pearly king. In her mind his face had a wide smile on it and she thought, for a moment, she could hear him as he said, "Hello, young lady, what can I do for you?"

Her eyes sprang open and she was faced with Long John Silver's head over the garden fence.

"Mum!" she said, sitting up, looking away from his direct stare.

"I said, I'm going to the garden centre. Is there anything I can get for you?"

Her mum, momentarily flustered, put on a warm smile.

"No, not at the moment, Eddie."

"See you then."

After he'd gone her mum said, "He's a nice man really. . ."

"That's not what you said to Dad last week!"

"You listen too much," her mum said. "He's just been unwell, that's all. Some sort of breakdown, probably. It's a pity he couldn't meet someone."

Maggie lay back on her chair. That was her mum's answer for most of the ills of the world. "If only he could meet someone".

The heat was becoming too much; she screwed her

nose up and pursed her lips. Getting up, she moved the deckchair a few feet back under the shade of an unruly bush. Her mum tutted.

"You'll never get a tan."

"It's bad for you anyroad," Maggie said and sat down again. Closing her eyes, she thought of Caroline.

When she'd been much younger the TV had brought odd stories into her life, children snatched in cars or from parks, enticed away by faceless men who had unclear motives for wanting them. At first Maggie had linked these stories to tales of kidnapping that she had read of or seen films about. She had assumed that ransom notes were probably sent to parents, demanding a sum of money for the safe return of their child. The men who took the children were just criminals looking for an easy way to make money.

But she had dropped this notion when reports came of dead bodies found, some minus their clothes, and TV reporters talking about a "serious sexual assault".

It had all been very confusing. Some time in her early years she had begun to associate "sex" with making babies. "Assaults" were about violence. Sex was something that happened between her parents. That had dawned on her somewhere between discarding her dolls and the present day. She hadn't just sat up and thought, my parents have sex; it hadn't happened like that. It had just become incorporated into her knowledge about the world.

But when a grey-faced TV man reported about the

finding of an eight-year-old boy or a six-year-old girl lying face down deep in the woods, Maggie was faced with a mystery. A child had been murdered. Sex was involved. It was like trying to fit together two pieces from different jigsaw puzzles.

It was when she was ten and she encountered the Material Man that other bits of the puzzle began to emerge.

A faint buzzing sounded in her ear and she swotted the air with her hand. When it continued she shifted about in the deckchair and finally she got up to move it about a bit.

"You're such a fidget!" her mum said, laughing. Maggie looked at her. Apart from talking to the man next door she hadn't moved for about two hours! The new baby was probably cooking in there.

"It's a wasp!" she said.

Maggie rolled up the newspaper and held it ready as a weapon.

It was a Thursday. That was the day her mum told her to go to the Material Man's shop.

"Go on your way home from school," her mum said. "You can catch him before he shuts for lunch. It's not out of your way."

Her mum had needed some special buttons that were the shape of small strawberries. The Material Man's shop sold everything from huge bales of tartan to tiny silver pins that had blue, red and yellow plastic balls on the end.

Her mum had always called him "the Material Man",

and at the time Maggie had conjured up an image of a man made entirely out of pieces of fabric. Satin skin and corduroy legs; a woollen top and gingham arms. On his face were sequins for the eyes and a piece of red felt cut out to make the lips. The nose was a silver thimble and his hair was the kind of fringe that usually hung from women's evening dresses.

When she'd gone into the shop with her mum from time to time she'd seen what he was really like: an old man with a round face and a round body which he mostly kept sitting on a chair behind the counter. Every now and then, if a customer asked, he took a deep breath and puffed up and down a small brown wooden ladder to get something.

In her head, though, Maggie had always thought of him in satins and ginghams, his eyes glittering, his felt lips cut in a perpetual smile.

On the day she went in he had aleady started to pack up for his early-closing day.

She'd dallied a bit at school, talking to her friends, and as she turned the corner into his street she'd realized that it was a minute or so till half past, when he was due to shut. She'd known that she would get into trouble if she missed him, and she ran and ran and ran until finally she burst through his door just as he was about to turn the sign around that said "Yes! We are open" to "Sorry! We are closed".

"What can I do for you, young lady?" he asked.

He walked back around the counter and sat down with a great exhalation of breath. In the couple of inches between the counter and his neck there seemed to be a mass of colour which she couldn't distinguish.

"My mum sent me," she said, taking great breaths herself. "She wants . . . she wants some of those . . . small buttons shaped like strawberries."

"Slow down, slow down. There's no rush," he said, smiling. "Are you in your lunch hour?"

"Yes," she smiled. It was then that she focused on the waistcoat. It was a silky garment with small coloured buttons sewn all over the front. There were leaves and flowers, giraffes and mice, cats and robins. There were dozens of tiny plain buttons that were cerise and tan and azure and tangerine, colours that she'd only seen in expensive eyeshadow boxes.

She'd been in his shop a number of times with her mum but she'd never seen the waistcoat before. He saw her looking at it.

"What do you think?" he said, beaming down at it.

"I think it's very nice," she said, and something caught her eye. At the corner, near the Material Man's rolled up shirtsleeve was a tiny button that looked like a diamond, or lots of minute diamonds stuck on to it.

He followed her eyes.

"Marcasite," he said. "Come and look," and he pushed his chair back from the counter.

She'd walked around the counter without thinking, looking closer at the diamond button.

"Here," he said, and, taking it in his two fingers, he ripped it from the waistcoat.

"Oh no," she said. She'd made him spoil his waistcoat. She shouldn't have looked at it. Her mum would be annoyed.

But there it was in his hand, like an expensive jewel, and she'd been the one that made him pull it off.

"Here," he said, patting his plump knees. "Come and sit here and I'll tell you about this jewel."

Why she had sat on his knee, she'd never known. Her mother afterwards had asked her over and over, *Why did you sit on his knee?* He'd asked her. He was a nice old man with an interesting waistcoat; he had a beautiful button in his hand; she had always been told to be polite to grown-ups, say thank you, say please. He had been pleasant to her; he had asked her to sit on his knee.

At the police station she hadn't remembered much about the story. Something about a princess losing an expensive diamond in her long satin evening dress. It had slipped off her neck and down the front among her taffeta petticoats, her lace camisole.

He had dropped the marcasite button down the front of her school shirt and felt for it on top of her clothes, just as the prince had done, down her buttons, across the pleats of her skirt, his hand rubbing across her front, back and forward and back and forward, his breath hot on her ear.

She had smiled with embarrassment; she didn't know what else to do.

"Where's that button?" he whispered again and again, and she could smell the tobacco off his breath as his hand slid on to her bare leg and moved up and down her thigh.

She'd laughed because his voice was light, as though he was making a joke. She'd looked to the door and watched out through the glass at the buses pulling up at their stop on the high road and people walking along as though nothing unusual was happening. As the rubbing continued she'd kept a smile on her face, but there was a heaviness in her chest. He'd taken the button off his waistcoat for her and was telling her a story but she didn't like the feel of his hand across her chest, across her stomach, on her thigh.

"I better go," she said lightly, but somewhere in the back of her throat she could feel a lump forming.

"I haven't finished the story yet," he said, and her eyes began to mist and she got a distorted view of the giraffes and the mice and garish turquoises and pinks that were in between. And his hand kept moving up and down up and down on her leg and then across her tummy, across her pants.

She'd jumped up and run round to the other side of the counter.

"I have to go," she said bobbing up and down on the spot, not sure whether to continue the politeness or just leave. In the silence of the shop and as she watched the Material Man take a deep breath and pull himself up out of the chair, she heard a "ping".

At her feet was the marcasite button, spinning slightly from its fall, shining on the floor. She looked at it with guilt, as though it was something she had stolen from him, as though she had been shoplifting and he had caught her at it.

He was moving slowly round the counter towards her. The same height as her on the chair, he now seemed like a giant, each step requiring a deep breath.

She turned and grabbed the door handle, ran out of the shop, up along the street and home.

Her mum was folding her chair up. She'd had enough sun.

Maggie wanted to ask her what had happened to him; where the Material Man had gone after he'd left the area; whether anyone had heard of him recently. But she stopped herself; they'd been over and over the whole thing in the years after it happened. It wasn't worth the upset it might cause, especially the way her mum was now.

SEVEN

Amy Cullen was standing outside Maggie's house when she got back from a trip to the shops. Leaning against a wall a few feet away was John. He was looking straight at her. Maggie felt herself flush and was about to hook her finger under the side of her bra when Amy said, "Developments. Follow me," and started to walk off up the street.

"Hang on," said Maggie. One of the things she really hated about Amy was the way she took charge of things. She was only ten!

"What?" Amy turned round and stood with her hands on her hips. Her face had metamorphosed into that of a sulky adolescent. Maggie looked at John. No chance of him saying anything.

"What developments?" Maggie sighed, transferring her carrier bag from one hand to the other.

"I can't say here," Amy said. "Make up your mind. You coming down the park or not?"

Maggie had an inclination to tell Amy to get stuffed.

It was eleven o'clock though; Maggie had an empty day stretching ahead of her and a letter to write to Bridget. She'd jotted down a list of topics to include in the letter but she still had the difficult business of putting it all into words. The prospect was torturous.

She looked at John, standing gazing across the street, his face vacant. If only she really was attracted to him. Then she'd have something to write about.

"God! I haven't got all day," Amy said with exasperation.

"I'll just get rid of this bag then," Maggie said, defeated. She addressed herself pointedly to John, even though he was miles away, not even looking at her.

Inside, her mum was sitting at the kitchen table, sorting through a shoebox of old photographs. She had her legs up on two cushions, so that her feet were higher than her bottom.

"Look at this!" she said, handing Maggie a photograph.

Maggie put the shopping down and took the print. It was a photograph taken at a wedding they had all been to some years ago. Her mum was on one side, her dad on the other. She stood in the middle, only up to her mum's shoulder, her dad's arm around her, all three of them with half-moon smiles, looking straight at the camera.

"I'm just going out," Maggie said, but she stood for a minute looking at the picture in her hand.

"And here's you when you were still in nappies." Her mum handed her a stiff cardboard frame. The words, "Maggie 13 months old" were written in what looked like her dad's handwriting.

A chubby baby smiled up from the picture. She was wearing a stiff yellow dress that seemed to stick out from the waist like a tutu. Underneath, Maggie could see the padding of the nappy, the short chubby legs sticking out at odd angles.

"This is the kind of photo me and your dad will show to the first boy that you bring home."

"Mum!" Maggie said. A picture of John Cullen jumped into her head and she put the photos down.

As she walked back up the hall she could hear her mum humming a song.

"I won't be long," she shouted, wishing she hadn't agreed to go and meet Amy.

When she got to the park John and Amy were sitting on adjacent swings. John was chewing and Amy had a cigarette in her hand and was fiddling with a box of matches while trying to keep the swing steady.

What a strange pair they made. John Cullen, ungainly, sitting on the swing like an overgrown schoolboy. Amy, his sister, her ten-year-old face and her twenty-five-year-old habits. It was as though they'd done a personality switch. One night Amy had gone to bed like a shy, boring young girl and John had dozed off with his hormones in turmoil, his character tossed to and fro on a sea of moods, his one desire to do all the things everyone had told him not to.

The next morning they had woken up as each other.

It wasn't such a silly fantasy, Maggie thought, watching Amy taking a long drag on her cigarette and her brother's eyes following a ball game a few yards away.

"What developments?" Maggie said in a businesslike way, standing far enough away from the pair so that no one would think she was with them.

"It was something Mary told me," Amy said, looking far across the park.

"Mary?" Maggie said. Mary Mitchell was Caroline's mum. It was another thing that annoyed her about Amy, the way she took to calling adults by their first names.

"Caroline's mum," John said suddenly. He had been listening, taking it all in.

"I know who she is!" Maggie was beginning to get exasperated. "*What* did she say?"

"Police found one of her trainers."

"Where?"

"In Lousy Park, down by the old sheds," John said, pushing his swing back as far as his legs would stretch and then letting it go so that he whooshed past Maggie.

"*No!*" Amy turned to her brother. "She never said the old sheds. She said near the old tyre factory."

"That's near the sheds."

"Not that near," Amy said holding her cigarette between her fingers as though it was a dart she was about to throw. Maggie felt a chill; it was only a few days ago that they had been down at Lousy Park.

"What about the trainer?" she said. "Never mind where they found it."

"Never mind where they found it!" Amy said, a look of disdain on her face. "That's great, that is. How are the police meant to find the body if they don't know exactly where they found the trainer!"

"I didn't mean that, I meant what about the trainer. Where is the other one? Were there any fingerprints on it?"

"You want to know a lot!" Amy was turning nasty.

"Who told Mrs Mitchell? Did they tell her anything else? What does it prove?" Finding the trainer seemed to raise more questions than it answered.

"Don't ask me," Amy said finally, lighting up another cigarette. "What do I know? I just know they found a shoe. No one else knows that, not the papers, not the neighbours, no one but Mary, me and now you."

Maggie noticed that she'd left out John. He didn't seem bothered.

"But that's not enough for you. It's not as if you've ever brought any information to this investigation, is it? What have you ever brought?" Amy made it sound as if the investigation had been going on for months and months.

In spite of a sense that it was all ridiculous, Maggie was beginning to feel angry.

"Your stuck-up friend goes away to Ireland so you hang around with me. In the past you turned your nose up at me and Caroline." Amy let the swing sway back and forward and, puckering up her lips as if she were about to say oooo, she blew a perfectly formed smoke ring into the air.

Maggie was speechless. She looked at Gormless John and his sister. What was she doing with this pair? How had she got into this?

"In the first place you *asked* me to come along, and in the second I do have some information that pertains to the disappearance!" The words leapt out before she had time to think. As soon as she'd spoken she felt silly. Pertains to the disappearance . . . who did she think she was?

"What?" Amy's face was still sulky but her body had tensed and the swing had come to a halt and was held still by her foot on the ground.

"I'm not telling a kid like you," Maggie said. In fact she wasn't quite sure what it was she had to tell.

"You know nothing," John said dismissively. "You don't know a thing." His swing had almost stopped its back and forward motion. Maggie was surprised for a minute at the certainty in his voice.

"What do you mean?" she said, miffed. How did he know she didn't have any information? It was one thing Amy shooting her mouth off. What did John know?

"That's as much as you know!" she said, feeling newly insulted by John's dismissal. "It just so happens that I heard the man next door crying in the middle of the night a few days ago."

"Yes?" Amy was sitting forward, her cigarette resting on the chain of the swing.

"And –" Maggie wasn't sure what she was going to say – "I saw him up at the Hollow Ponds when they were dragging them."

"Yes?" Amy's face was in a state of frozen anticipation. John Cullen was looking down at his lap and was just starting a yawn when Maggie felt panic. Why had she started this? What did she know? She'd only linked Long John to Caroline because at first she'd thought that Caroline had been the one doing the crying. She couldn't tell them that. What kind of story would that make?

"Is that all!" Amy said derisively. Maggie looked at John, who seemed to be mouthing the words of a song. She'd lost his attention.

"And he's an ex-mental patient! I heard my mum and dad say it. He's only just come out. He's been in there ten years!" Amy, just in the course of putting her cigarette in her mouth, stood up off her swing.

"A mental patient!" she said.

"And he's got a black car. Isn't that what you said, John? That Caroline got into a black car?"

"Ten years," Amy said softly.

"So just add all that up," Maggie said, feeling her confidence grow.

"Perhaps he was crying with guilt," Amy said to no one in particular.

"A trainer!" Maggie threw a laugh carelessly into the air. "What does that tell us?"

"Up at the ponds. So maybe she is up there then." Amy sat down on her swing again, her face softened. "Well, fancy that!" she said.

EIGHT

Maggie was looking out of her mum and dad's bedroom window. Amy and John were sitting on the wall of the flats. Long John was walking up the street past them.

In a kind of silent movie, Maggie watched as Amy got up and walked after Long John, dragging her leg behind her in just the way that he did. She walked a few steps and he suddenly turned round. In a flash, Amy resumed a completely normal walk, doing a U-turn and joining her brother back on the wall. Long John stood for a moment and then turned and went off up the street.

Amy and John started to laugh.

Maggie felt remorse settle like a stone on her stomach.

She went into her own bedroom and resumed writing her letter to Bridget. So far she had written that Caroline was still missing and the man next door was a gardener. It was dull and she had used the minimum of words.

It wasn't that she didn't have things to say: she could have described the day over at Lousy Park; she could have told her about hanging around with John and Amy; she could have explained why she had exposed Long John to Amy and John's ridicule.

It was all so complicated, though. None of these topics were straightforward. Bridget would be astonished if she knew that Maggie was hanging around with the Cullens;

she would laugh at her, particularly if she said that John seemed to like her, "fancy" her even. She wouldn't understand what it was like to be deserted by her best friend; to be completely alone day after day; to have letters that showed what a full and exciting time her best friend was having without her.

Then there was poor Long John; she hadn't lied about him but she'd told it in such a way that the whole thing sounded mysterious. And why had she done it? In order to impress Amy and John Cullen.

She had suggested his involvement and now Amy and John were convinced he was the abductor. If he ever became a "suspect", it would be her responsibility.

How could she explain all that to Bridget?

She picked up the pad and wrote, *The police have found one of Caroline's trainers down in Lousy Park. Will write again soon. Love Maggie*. It would have to do.

Maggie looked at her watch. It was eleven thirty, time she went to meet the others.

"I think we should watch him. We could make out a rota. Maggie, you could watch late at night from your window. I could do the mornings. John could do the afternoons."

"Watch him!" Maggie said. "We're not private detectives, you know!"

John spoke: "We could write an anonymous letter to the police."

"That would be awful." Maggie felt herself going red. Long John would be dragged into the police station, perhaps charged with something he didn't do, all because of what she said.

"Nah," Amy said, "we've got no evidence. We need to watch him. So that we can build up evidence."

"We could write to the newspapers. Get them involved." John was being particularly verbal for once. Maggie wished he would keep quiet.

"You know what the newspapers are like; they print loads of lies!" Maggie felt desperation creeping into her voice.

"But this isn't lies," John said.

"We've got no evidence," Amy said and there was silence.

It was time for Maggie to withdraw her accusations. The whole thing was getting out of hand. Anonymous letters; newspaper reporters; the police; it was all too much.

She should simply explain how she'd blown it all out of proportion.

"Look," she said.

"I'll draw up a rota," Amy interrupted. 'We'll watch him for a while. If there's any hard evidence then we'll write a letter to the police."

"I. . ." Maggie was trying to find the words to confess but suddenly there was no need. If they were going to wait until they had hard evidence in order to expose Long John, then there was no need for her to say anything. There would be no evidence. In a few days the whole thing would be forgotten.

"You do late at night," Amy said. Maggie hated being ordered about by Amy but for once she kept quiet. It was the best way; let Amy and John think that she was as keen as them. Then when they saw nothing and heard nothing they would give it up.

"We're going over the ponds this afternoon," Amy said. "Want to come?"

"No," Maggie said. She didn't have anything to do but it was time she distanced herself from these two. It was time she found other things to do to pass the time until Bridget returned.

"See you then," John said, looking straight at her.

She smiled and nodded, but inside her head she thought, not if I see you first.

NINE

Maggie's mother was kneeling over the toilet. Her face looked white and she was gasping for breath.

"I'll ring Dad!" Maggie said with exasperation.

"No." Her mother had her hands clasped loosely on the plastic toilet seat and she rested her forehead on them. For a moment she looked to Maggie as though she were deep in prayer.

"He told me to!" Maggie said quietly, almost in a whisper.

"I'll be all right," her mother said, "just give me a minute."

Maggie sat on the edge of the bath and rubbed her mother's shoulders. After a minute or so, she said, "Come and have a lie down on the bed."

"One glass of red wine. That was all I had. The last time I felt like this I'd drunk a litre bottle all by myself!" her mum said, standing up slowly. Maggie felt her hand trembling as it leant on her arm.

"I'll just lie for a while," her mum said. "You get me some water, will you, love?"

"I'll get you some wine if you like," Maggie said, smiling half-heartedly.

As she walked down the stairs Maggie could hear her retching again. She stood still for a moment, fear gathering in her stomach. What if it was a sign that the baby was coming? She was in the house alone with her mum. What if the baby came too quickly to get her mum into hospital?

There was no question in her mind. She ought to ring her dad. Her dad ought to know what was going on. Hadn't he said exactly that the previous evening?

She'd gone into the kitchen with him while her mum was watching TV.

"Promise me you'll ring me if anything seems unusual. Anything at all. You know what she's like," he'd said, pointing with his thumb to the wall that divided the kitchen from the front room. "You know how she'll leave everything to the last minute. She hates doctors."

"But you know what she's like as well!" Maggie had said. "I can't make her do anything."

"Course you can," he'd said, smiling. "You and her, thick as thieves."

Maggie had frowned.

"Hey, come on," he'd said, hugging her. "I'm depending on you to look after her."

Later she'd found three one pound coins on her bedside cabinet. She'd just finished looking out of the window towards Long John's back door when she'd noticed them there: three sand-coloured circles, two at the bottom and one on top, like the beginnings of a pyramid. She'd swept them off into her tin where they joined the rest. She replaced the lid and shook the tin to hear the rattle of the money; it gave her a feeling of guilt and she closed the money away in a drawer, still unspent, payment for work she had never done.

And this morning, with her mum being sick as a dog in the bathroom, there was work she could have done. She could have rung her dad. She stood by the phone in the hall, her fingers tapping on the receiver with indecision when she heard, "Don't you ring your father," from upstairs.

She went into the kitchen and put the kettle on.

Some time later she heard her mum's footsteps coming down the stairs. There was a "thwack" sound as each of her strapless sandals hit the soles of her feet. Maggie went out into the hall.

"I'm just going to the doctor's. He told me to call in if I felt unwell. I'll be back soon."

"But. . ." Maggie looked at her mum and then at the phone. She should ring her dad.

"Why don't you come along?" Her mum stood by the door. "Then you won't need to report me to Dad. You can personally look after me."

"OK," Maggie said.

"One thing." Her mum opened the front door.

"Yes?" Maggie hoped she wasn't going to ask her to keep it all a secret from her dad.

"Don't ever give me a glass of red wine again."

In the afternoon she found John Cullen on his own over the back of the flats. She'd been avoiding him and his sister for days. She wondered if they'd noticed. He was sitting on the ground leaning back against the wall, his legs spread open, a comic lying flat on the tarmac.

"Hi," she said. If he asked she could always say she'd been looking after her mum.

"Um," he said, continuing to read.

"Where's Amy?" she said. They probably hadn't even noticed her absence.

"Dunno," he said. He didn't lift his eyes off the comic.

She sat down beside him. "Thought you were on reconnaissance." She said it sarcastically. It wasn't that she was bothered whether he was watching Long John or not. It was just something to say.

He turned and gave her a disdainful look. "Got better things to do."

She raised her eyebrows; she'd thought he was more bothered about it than that.

"I think I was on the wrong track anyroad," Maggie said. Maybe she could gently retrieve the whole situation.

"No," John said. "No, I still think it could be him. The more I think about that black car, the more I think it was his. It had a flimsy front. I said to the police at the time, it was an old-fashioned black motor."

"Well. . ." Maggie started. She was about to say that the police had already visited him, but John Cullen continued.

"That's where they send them, you know. Child molesters, perverts. They don't send them to the nick, they send them to mental hospitals. Sometimes they stay there all their lives."

Maggie's mouth opened to speak but nothing came out. She looked for a moment at John Cullen's profile. He looked different, older in some way. His face seemed to have sunk into his neck and he was staring across the flats and into the streets beyond. There was something sad about him. Sometimes he seemed so grown up, like that day on his bike up at Hollow Ponds. Then other times he was like an overgrown kid, like when he was running away from Amy down at Lousy Park. She remembered his arm around her waist when they were hiding.

She wanted to ask him what he knew about mental hospitals when she noticed his shoes.

"You've got new trainers," she said.

"Um," he said and he looked straight at her for a moment. Averting her eyes with embarrassment she said, "They're nice."

"Yes," he said, got up and walked off towards the flats.

She uncrossed her legs and stood up, unsure whether to follow him. He even looked different as he walked away, more stocky, his walk more determined than usual.

"See you later," she shouted, but he didn't turn round.

"The trouble is," Amy said, taking a long yellow chip and pushing it into her mouth, "unless we get inside that house we'll never know whether he is really implicated or not." Maggie looked at Amy. "Implicated" was a big word. She was surprisingly articulate at times.

"Where's John?" Maggie said.

"Dunno," said Amy, taking two chips at once. Maggie could smell the vinegar and began to feel the faint rumblings of hunger even though she'd only had her tea an hour or so previously.

"We could break in there," Amy said, her face blank. Maggie looked at her with amazement. It was as if she'd just said, we could go swimming or we could go to the pictures; she had used the same tone of voice.

"Don't be ridiculous." Maggie took a deep breath. It was time for her to exercise her authority in terms of years and explain to Amy about the law and Morality in general. Amy's voice distracted her thoughts.

"We could wait until he goes out then one of us could stand outside and keep guard. We could get over your back wall – you said his back door's open night and day – and go in. It's not as if we're burglars. We're not going to damage the place and we're not going to steal anything. We're doing it for a good cause. The police do it all the time. We could take a room each and search carefully and when we're done we could come back out. No one would know except us and if we do find something then it's because he's guilty and he's done away with Caroline. And if it turns out that he's not, then we meant well."

"You just can't," Maggie was about to respond, to explain, to inform Amy of what was right and what was wrong, but Amy had seen one of her friends across the street and had walked off and left her standing in the middle of the pavement, her mouth open.

It was the second time that day she had been left standing by a Cullen. She tutted loudly and, using two hands, pulled her bra down.

"Housebreaking," she said out loud, and started to walk towards home.

TEN

At twelve the next day Maggie found herself sitting in the small kitchen of number fifty. Beside her on the table was half a glass of fizzy orange. Maggie looked at her watch. She'd only been there for thirty minutes and yet it seemed like hours.

"Huh," she said. The word seemed to linger in the air for a few seconds and she imagined Amy Cullen's face if she knew where she was now. So much for housebreaking. Here Maggie was, sitting in the very house Amy was desperate to get into, and she hadn't had to lift a devious finger to get there.

Her mother had said earlier that morning, "Eddie's got his weekly appointment at the clinic. He's bought a fridge and he needs someone to sit in and wait for it. Do you mind? Just for an hour or so. He's such a nice man and some of the kids from the flats are giving him a hard time."

"Who do you mean?" Maggie had said it guiltily, knowing full well who it was.

"Oh, I don't know. Some of those kids. He says they make faces at him when he's walking up the street. He's sure one of them has scratched his car. I dare say he's just a bit sensitive, what with his illness."

"What exactly is his illness?" Maggie had said.

Her mum sat down in the chair opposite her.

"Truth is I don't really know. Mrs Rogers said he'd had a breakdown. You know, when someone can't cope with what's happening in their life. People have painful experiences or their circumstances become so difficult to live with that their minds just kind of turn off."

Maggie swallowed a lump of guilt quietly. This was the man that she'd thrown to Amy and John. She'd gathered up her magazines and walked next door.

"Hello, Mr Young," she said brightly, when he opened the door. In her head she pictured him for a moment with a cocked hat and a patch over one eye.

He took her into the kitchen.

"There's fizzy orange," he said, and pointed to the table. Maggie was about to answer when he continued, "And there's the glasses." Maggie nodded, waiting for him to speak again. After what seemed like a very long time he said, "And biscuits are in the cupboard."

"Right," Maggie said crisply, wanting him to go.

"Are you sure," he said, and looked around the kitchen slowly, "you don't mind?"

"Certain," Maggie said, sitting down and laying her magazines on the table. For a minute she wondered if he might be drunk. His words were mildly slurred. Eventually he'd turned to go.

"I'll be off then."

He didn't go though. Maggie sat for five or so minutes while he told her about the house. His words were slow and Maggie had trouble keeping eye contact with him as he spoke. His eyelids looked heavy but there was no smell of alcohol from him. When he finally went she shrugged her shoulders. It was probably the drugs her mum said he had to take.

She reached across for the bottle of fizzy orange. Why did adults always think young people preferred fizzy drinks? She would have liked a cup of tea.

The kitchen was long and thin. There was an old-fashioned sink unit and an old geyser on the wall which he must use for hot water. There were no fitted cupboards, no tiles on the wall, no microwave or food processor. There was a small wooden cupboard with a flap that came down as a worktop. It looked like it came from a junk shop. It was painted blue and the flap had some sticky-backed plastic stuff on it.

Maggie picked up the lukewarm orange. He certainly needed a fridge.

She wondered what the rest of the house was like. He'd told her to be careful if she went upstairs to the toilet, as a lot of the floorboards had been taken out because they were rotten.

He obviously lived in the downstairs rooms. He had said he was renovating the house. Apart from some holes in the wall where plaster had fallen out Maggie couldn't see any evidence of woodwork or decoration.

She imagined for a moment Amy searching through the cupboard with the flap, looking behind the bottle of tomato ketchup or the packet of sugar. Amy would no doubt go upstairs and look under the floorboards thinking that Long John had left clues there.

Ridiculous!

Maggie got up and walked out of the kitchen into the hallway. She turned the handle of the front-room door and went in, intending just to look out of the window in case the fridge men were coming.

It was furnished like a bed-sitting room. There was a small TV in one corner and a bed against the wall opposite. An old-fashioned chest of drawers sat in the bay of the window and by the foot of the bed was a steel rail for hanging clothes. A black suit hung on a wooden hanger and beside it on a wire hanger was a white ironed shirt. Draped over the top of the rail was a plain black tie. There were no other clothes hung up. Perhaps Long John had a wardrobe in another room.

Pulling aside the net curtain Maggie looked for a delivery van. There was none. Maggie felt tempted to open the drawers and take a peek. She had no intention of moving anything about inside them but she was just interested to see what kind of things the man had.

No, it wasn't fair. She'd hate it if anyone went rummaging round in her cupboards, even though there were only old toys and comics crushed in there.

It wouldn't be nice. She'd only come into this room to look out of the window. It wasn't as if she was Amy Cullen after all. She turned and closed the door quietly behind her.

The door of the back sitting room was a foot or two away.

In Maggie's house the two downstairs rooms had been

knocked into one and the door of the back room had been removed and the hole plastered over so as to look as though it was just part of the wall.

Long John's door handle had come off and there was only the spoke sticking out. It was dangerous really, if there had been a small child in the house it might have had its eye put out.

She wondered how big the room looked. Her mum had filled that area with a dining room set and some shelves that held china. What had the room looked like before her dad had taken the bricks away?

That was why she turned the spoke and let the door click open. She wasn't searching for anything, as Amy would have done. She was seeing what her front room used to look like.

The room had been decorated. The walls were white and there was a square of carpet on the floor. There was a desk over by the small window but apart from that no other furniture at all. She walked across to look out towards the garden. She wanted to see if Long John could see her bedroom from here.

It was when she was standing by the desk that she turned to look at the adjacent wall, the one with the door in, the one she hadn't looked at as she'd stood gazing around the room.

It was covered in photographs.

The wall was white and all the photographs were in black and white, not colour. Maggie stood still at the desk looking up and down the wall, from side to side, from corner to corner. There were maybe fifteen or twenty photographs on the wall, all black and white.

Fifteen or twenty photographs all of the same girl. Maggie said "Huh" again and heard the sound echo in the emptiness of the room. She remembered when she and Bridget had been mad about some singer or other and had collected all of the photographs of him they could get their hands on. Maggie had covered her bedroom wall with his grinning face, his long body, his pouting poses.

But this! Maggie leant back on the desk, feeling dismay. Not only were they photos of the same girl but they were all the same photo. The face of a young girl smiling into the camera. Some of the photos were blown up, one so much so that it was blurred out of recognition. Some looked as small as passport photos and some the size that might sit in a wooden frame on the mantelpiece or shelves.

What would Amy make of this, Maggie wondered. It was just as well she wasn't here now. Whatever reason Long John had for keeping these photos, Amy would be sure to twist it, exaggerate it, distort it.

But what reason could he have for such a display?

Maggie wanted to sit down but there was no chair. She lowered her bottom and sat on the floor looking at the faces of the girl on the wall opposite.

Perhaps he was some kind of arty photographer. Or a painter? They sometimes used photographs.

It didn't seem likely. There was no gear anywhere that she could see.

She stood up and gently opened the desk drawer. If he

was an artist he'd have his brushes and pencils stored away somewhere. The drawer was empty. She opened the other side drawer. It was also empty. Of the two lower drawers one was missing and the other had no handle. Kneeling down, she reached her arm underneath the desk to the back of the drawer and with an effort pushed it so that it opened about half an inch. Catching her breath, she sat back on her legs. Anyone looking might have thought she was kneeling down about to pray.

She glanced sideways at the photos again. When she had had her pictures covering her bedroom wall her mum had said she was obsessed with the man. She had liked the sound of that word, "obsessed". She had taken the word over and used it in conversations at school saying, dramatically, that she had an absolute obsession with something or other. She didn't just use it about people, she used it about sweets, clothes, magazines, anything that she vaguely liked.

In the end it had just disappeared from her conversation, filed away in some cerebral limbo, waiting to be used at some other time.

The drawer was inching open and Maggie had to reach down and shove the back of it as hard as she could a couple of times.

Obsession. She could use the word now. Whoever the girl on the wall was, Long John certainly had an obsession with her.

A final shove from the back and the drawer edged open enough to see inside.

At first all she could see were a variety of shapes and colours muted by the shadows of the room. She put her hand in and started to take things out. Not thinking, almost holding her breath, she laid the items out in a semicircle around her on the floor.

There were some colourful ribbons, the kind that young kids have in their hair, and some patterned slides. There was a small T-shirt with a faded beach scene on it. There was a small purse with brightly coloured beads attached to it. Next she picked out three paperback books, grubby, their pages beginning to yellow. They were Enid Blyton books, two Secret Seven and one Malory Towers.

Then she picked out a small grubby stuffed animal. It was in the shape of a rabbit and its eyes were embroidered on instead of the usual glass beads. It was very old and parts of its fur fabric had been worn away by constant touching.

She picked up a pair of socks and a flimsy petticoat.

She didn't stop, as she was laying these things around her on the floor, to guess at who might own them. There were no voices in her head that linked the objects with the bizarre pictures on the wall to her side but she began to feel uneasy all the same.

Putting her hand in the drawer she came upon the only thing left. It was a plastic bag with something inside. She gripped and it felt soft, like a collection of strands of wool or cotton laid together. She opened the bag slowly, not sure of what it would be, glancing quickly at the wall opposite and the circle of items spaced around her like some mystical spell that she was trying to cast. The girl's face smiled across at her as she shook the bag and let the contents fall on to the floor.

At first she felt herself jump slightly and said "Ah" so softly that she hardly heard it. There was a knot in her chest as she looked at a girl's plait of hair lying like a dead snake on the floor in front of her. She put her hand out to touch it but recoiled. It lay on the floor in an "S" shape, about seven inches of thick brown hair, loosely plaited and fastened at both ends with elastic bands. She stretched her hand out and touched it with her index finger, ready to jump back should it feel alien or strange.

The hair felt dry and hard. Relaxing, she picked it up and held it in her hand. Its lightness surprised her and she stroked it a couple of times with her other hand, as though it was some tiny animal.

There she was kneeling, a semicircle of childhood paraphernalia around her, stroking a disembodied plait of hair, when the ring of the doorbell seemed to stab into the silence.

She jumped up.

It couldn't be Long John. He had his own key.

She replaced the plait in the bag and put it and the other items carefully back in the drawer. With a last look at the smiling girl she went out of the room to answer the front door.

ELEVEN

"Listen to this." Maggie's mother was reading a magazine. It was breakfast time and they were sitting around the kitchen table. The back door was open and the sun threw a yellowy stripe across the shadows of the room. "There's a summer sale at Mothercare. Some buggies and pushchairs half-price!"

To the side of Maggie's cereal dish was a letter from Bridget. It was three folded-up pages and it read like a chapter of a book, long and detailed; it described a blossoming love affair between Bridget and her cousin Brendan.

"I don't have to be in work until late," her dad said. "We could take a run over to Wood Green. If you feel up to it."

Maggie picked Bridget's letter up again and let the conversation at the table become a blur at the back of her head. Bridget had been out with Brendan and his friends on and off since she'd arrived in Ireland. A few days ago she'd been out with him alone and in the letter Bridget outlined exactly what they'd spent their time doing.

Maggie had felt a degree of embarrassment when she'd read the details. She'd tried to picture Bridget and her cousin, whatever he looked like, on their date. She'd tried to imagine the pair of them doing the things that Bridget had described.

There was also a niggling frustration. It had hardly taken any time for Bridget to replace her, while she was stuck in London with nobody.

Maggie felt a burgeoning gloom. Bridget was having the time of her life yet she found time to write pages and pages to Maggie. Maggie seemed to move like a tortoise through the long empty hours of each day, yet she couldn't manage more than a few lines.

This irony made her lean against the back of her chair. She looked towards her mum and dad, who were at the other end of the table, a few feet away. They were talking quietly about something.

On top of her virtual isolation she now had new things to worry about. In her head she had imagined herself writing it all down on a crisp white piece of paper to Bridget. She could almost see a pen writing in a neat sloped script.

The man next door, an ex-mental patient, had a room in his house full of young girl's things. In this room there was a wall covered in photographs of a young girl. It was the same photograph reproduced over and over again.

A few weeks ago, when this man moved into the area, a young girl had gone missing and had never been seen since. She was seen getting into an old black car like the one the man next door had. He was seen skulking around the Hollow Ponds when they were searching for her body. He had been heard crying bitterly in the middle of the night; in fear of being caught, Amy Cullen had suggested.

The photographs weren't of Caroline Mitchell, though;

they were of some other young girl, some stranger.

It ought to have been easy to write to Bridget, to tell her all about it.

Then there was the plait of hair. In her head Maggie saw it lying on the floor, its strands uniformly entwined, looking like a length of luxurious rope. Maggie felt as though she was going to shiver and she braced her shoulders. It wasn't unusual for girls to have their long hair cut. Some girls even kept the piece that had been taken off, especially if it had been very long.

Her mum and dad were still talking, although the blur in Maggie's head had taken on a sharper, more determined sound. They were probably making plans again, for the nursery or the christening, or just another shopping trip.

Where had Long John got that plait of hair? And the other things?

Her mother laughed out loud at something. If only she could tell her what she had found in Long John's. What a sense of relief that would give her.

She remembered then, with a feeling of unease, the last time she had strung a list of facts together about Long John. True, she had had questionable motives for telling Amy and John what she'd seen and as soon as she'd laid them all out she'd felt bad about it. Once out of her mouth, she'd seen it for the concocted story it had been and Long John looked as innocent as a baby. Amy and John had picked it up differently, though; to them it had all joined together and formed a big arrow which pointed towards him. Thankfully, their interest seemed to have waned in the last few days and they had left him alone. She'd ended up feeling mean. What if she now described what she had seen in his house? What kind of furore would that start?

Her mum was different, though. She wouldn't blow things out of proportion.

Maggie looked across at her mother. Her huge lump was causing her to sit away from the edge of the table and lean across on her elbows. She had no make-up on and her face looked round and shiny, her mouth open slightly, the corners of her eyes creased in a half-smile.

She pictured her face the night that Caroline had gone missing, tears smudging her mascara, her mouth pursed into a small crooked line.

It wasn't worth upsetting her with something she wasn't sure about.

Her dad was the one to tell.

She looked across at him.

It would be difficult to sit and tell him all the things that had happened.

Her dad was great at fixing things, like her headphones when they went wrong, or the shelf in her bedroom when it started to come away from the wall. He was really brilliant when it came to taking things back to shops to get a refund, like the skirt she'd bought that had come apart at the waistband. He always knew the answers to general knowledge questions on quiz shows and he made her laugh when he imitated the voices of politicians or posh people they overheard in shopping centres.

But she couldn't remember ever having confided in him without her mum knowing. It was hard to imagine what it might be like to sit and have a long conversation with him unless her mum was there, filling up the gaps and explaining things when she didn't know what to say.

"You could come if you want, Maggie." Her mum's voice cut into her thoughts.

"No, thanks," she said, pushing her cereal bowl away. Maybe she'd tell him when she'd thought about it a bit more.

She was about to pick up Bridget's letter but decided to leave it there; it would serve her right if some adult picked it up and read it.

Maggie pulled the duvet across to make her bed and then flopped down on top of it.

Bridget had a boyfriend!

She had a moment of panic. Bridget was her best friend. They had been together as long as she could remember. She lived a couple of streets away and they had met at primary school. They grew up liking the same pop groups and wore the same fashions when they could afford it. People in school got used to saying Maggie and Bridget, or Bridget and Maggie.

Bridget in Ireland for six weeks! They'd first heard about the proposed trip at Easter, when her relatives came over for a short holiday. Bridget and her mother had been invited to go for the entire school holidays.

At first Bridget had been horrified. Six weeks staying at a farm in the middle of Waterford. There was no electricity, no running water, no cinemas, no nothing. It was like being sent to Siberia, she said.

Maggie had been in Bridget's bedroom when she'd heard her running up the stairs. The door had flown open and Bridget had dramatically thrown herself on the bed. Her sobs had been fervent and loud. Maggie had tried to shush her and tell her that it wouldn't be so bad. Deep inside she had been pleased. Bridget's parents were not hard; they wouldn't force her to go.

Bridget's mother had come in. Nobody was going to force Bridget to go. In the end it would be her own choice; but Bridget had got it all wrong, she'd said. There had been running water at the farm for fifty or more years. They'd had an inside bathroom and shower room installed in the five years since she'd been. Bridget's sobs subsided a little at that. A shower room? she'd said. The farm had had electricity for thirty years or more, her mother had gone on. In the past year they'd had central heating put in and they now had two TVs and a video. A video? Bridget said. Both her sisters had their own cars and in the nearest town, which was seven miles away, there was a cinema and a McDonald's and a lot of clothes shops. Bridget sat up on the bed and blew her nose into a large piece of kitchen roll. But no one would force Bridget to go. It would be her own choice.

Bridget's mother was sitting on the edge of the bed by that time. Nobody should forget, she said, the fairs that went round to please the tourists and the miles and miles of sandy beaches. The redness had gone from Bridget's face and there was a half-smile forming.

Then there's your cousin Brendan and all his pals. Enough there for a boyfriend or two, I shouldn't wonder, she had said, getting up.

There was no rush at all. Bridget could weigh it all up and let them know. They weren't about to book the tickets until the following weekend.

Maggie had been appalled. In a few short minutes she had lost Bridget to Waterford, which her mother had virtually likened to Las Vegas. She'd gone home almost in tears, feeling deserted, even though it was four months until Bridget had to go.

The next day Bridget's mum had rung her house. What would her mum and dad think if she accompanied Bridget and her mother to Ireland? Six weeks would be a long time but they would keep an eye on them both and she was sure Maggie would have a great time.

It was up to Maggie, her mum and dad had said. She should be the one to make the decision.

The fact that the three of them had never been parted for that long before shouldn't really be a factor, Maggie's mum had said. Maggie was responsible and had been doing things alone for a long time.

The cost of the return airfare and her spending money would be a lot. She would have to have new clothes, quite a few if she were going for six weeks. It could come to three or four hundred pounds, her dad had said. They were a bit stretched, it was true, but he thought he could get a loan from the bank. It would only mean a few pounds back every month.

It was Maggie's decision, they said.

But Maggie had looked at them with suspicion. She knew they didn't want her to go.

They said that she wasn't to worry about her mum's condition. Lots of women went through their final weeks of pregnancy alone, her mum had said; even women in their late thirties. Nine times out of ten nothing terrible happened. She could manage. And if anything was wrong Dad was only a phone call away.

Maggie had pictured her mum, alone in the house, not being able to get to the phone.

Then there was the new baby. When it was born, they had wanted her to be there. But it probably wouldn't make an ounce of difference if she didn't see it until it was a few weeks old. It would always be her brother or sister, after all, and small babies often didn't distinguish between adults around them anyway.

Maggie saw a family photograph: her mum, her dad and the new baby, a space in the middle where she should have been.

Maggie could take her time about deciding. Bridget's mum wasn't buying the tickets until the weekend.

Maggie had looked at each of her parents in turn, their faces full of innocence. She had found them out, though.

Four months later Maggie had helped Bridget pack. They'd write two or three times a week. Long letters full of details about what was going on. They wouldn't change, they'd still be best friends when Bridget came back. It would be as if she'd never been away.

But things were changing, Maggie could feel it. Already Bridget was doing things that Maggie had never done. Going out with boys! Bridget would come back an experienced woman and she, Maggie, would never even have been kissed.

If only Maggie had a boyfriend, if only she could write back describing her dates, her kisses, her experiences.

Her thoughts were interrupted by the sound of her parents in the hall downstairs and the front door opening. She could hear voices coming from the street and she walked into the front bedroom to look out of the window. There were a couple of police cars parked outside the flats and a small crowd was gathering around the entrance. She could see her mum trudging across the street, her dad following. To the side of one police car was John Cullen.

He was talking to one of the young policemen and for a moment she looked at him, ignoring the questions in her head about what was going on.

She wanted to go out on to the street but for once she wasn't really interested in what the commotion was about. She looked at herself in her mother's dressing-table mirror and, opening a drawer, took a brush and tidied her hair.

Taking her mum's perfume, she squirted a bit on her neck, her arms.

"What's happened? Have they found Caroline?" she said as she walked confidently up to him.

He turned and looked at her for a few seconds.

"No," he said, "they've got the bloke who took her though. He's in custody at this moment."

"That's good," she said, not really thinking about what he had said. "Are you doing anything tonight? Fancy going out somewhere; just you and me?"

TWELVE

They didn't actually go out.

"I'm broke," John had said when she walked to the corner to meet him, "but my mum's gone out with Amy over to her sister's. We can watch a video. They won't be back until tenish."

It gave them just under two hours.

They walked up the stairs of the flats in silence and Maggie noticed that John Cullen had the same clothes on that he'd been wearing earlier that day. He hadn't bothered to change.

She'd had a bath and washed her hair; she'd ironed her clean jeans and her top; she'd coated some black mascara on her eyelashes and put gel on her hair to make it stand out a bit.

She'd popped her head into the front room where her mum and dad were. She'd had to cough a bit to get their attention because her mum was taking deep breaths while her dad rubbed at her shoulders, saying, "Right down to the diaphragm. You can do it."

"You're ready then," her mum had said between inhalations.

"Have a nice time," her dad had said, following her along the hall. He gave her a pound coin as she went out of the front door.

She'd told them she was going to the pictures with some girls from school who lived nearby.

She could have told them she was going out with John Cullen. They wouldn't have minded. They were often throwing hints to her about boyfriends and dates.

The truth was that since her courageous invitation that morning she had got cold feet. She wasn't embarrassed or afraid of seeing him; she just didn't know whether she wanted to see him at all. Telling her parents would have given the evening much more importance than it should have.

Pausing at the top of the stairs as John Cullen searched through his pockets for keys to open the front door, Maggie wondered what to say to break the silence. After a few seconds she said, "Good about the police catching that bloke."

"Um," John said. He was pushing his hands down into his jeans, first one pocket, then the other.

"Mrs Rogers says he'd done it before. Apparently every time something happens to a kid the police pull in all the dirty old men in the area."

He still didn't reply.

"Have you lost the key?" Maggie said. His face had a look of intense concentration and his left hand was so far down his trousers that Maggie thought his pockets must have ended at his knee.

There was silence for a moment and Maggie watched as John Cullen's face looked first flustered and then irritated.

"I expect he'll confess soon and then her body will be

found," she said, wishing he would hurry up. "After all. . ."

"Got it!" John Cullen produced a small gold key from the depths of his jeans. "Thought Amy had it."

"A keyring's a good idea," Maggie couldn't help saying as she followed him into his flat.

The front room was surprisingly clean and tidy. For some reason Maggie had thought that it would be a mess.

"Where's your dad?" Maggie said.

"He works away. I'll see if there's anything to drink."

"Oh yeah," she said, grinning. "On the oil rigs."

When he was gone Maggie felt enveloped in disappointment. This wasn't what she had had in mind at all. What kind of story would it make? She and John sat in his front room watching a video all night. Where was the romance in that? Bridget and Brendan were probably walking hand in hand along some windswept beach at that very moment.

She heard John Cullen in the kitchen and felt a small shiver. He was so difficult to talk to. He didn't ever seem to laugh. It was all very well having new trainers, but what kind of evening would it be if they couldn't at least have a conversation?

He came back with two small glasses of lager. "We only had one tin," he said, and gave her a glass. She sipped it. She'd had lager before. It wasn't as nice as sparkling wine. A home video and half a can of lager. What would Bridget make of that?

"This video's great," he said, sitting cross-legged on the floor and pushing it into the machine. He got up and pulled the curtains shut to block out the evening light. Maggie sipped her lager and looked at him stepping back across the coffee table.

As he sat down he turned his head to face her and kissed her on the lips. Her neck tensed and her eyes opened. Blindly steering her hand she placed the glass of lager on the side table. He kept on kissing her, oblivious to her surprise. His mouth felt hard and, not knowing what to do, she puckered her lips to respond, as though she was kissing her dad. His lips and head kept moving about though, and in a second she realized that he wanted her to open her mouth. When she did, his tongue slid across her teeth and she could feel it moving, licking across the front of her gums. Her head was bent back against the settee and she had a kind of weak feeling in her chest.

Suddenly, without any warning, the kiss stopped and John Cullen turned back to face the screen.

Her mouth still hanging open, she stared for a minute at his profile. Putting her fingers up to her lips, she turned back towards the screen herself. How odd he was; one minute he was like a young man, the next like a kid.

They watched the film in silence for most of the time. It was set in the year 2020 and was about a number of street gangs in New York. There were a lot of young, white, black and brown men posing with flick knives and lengths of piping saying things like, "Yo man", "Hey dude", "My boy", "Watch your face, man."

Once or twice a woman walked across the action, her

face made up to perfection, her breasts spilling out of some tightly fitted top. Not really what you'd call a girl's film, Maggie thought. It was something she would have liked to say out loud but she sensed that it was a comment that would have dropped like a stone in the room.

Not that John Cullen would even have heard it. He sat rapt, completely absorbed in the film, as though kissing Maggie had been something somebody else had done. He moved to the edge of the seat, his elbows on his knees, his feet tapping the floor at fast fighting bits. Every now and then he said, "This bit's good. Watch. Watch", or, "He gets killed now, look see", or, "Look at that!"

Most of the film happened in the background of Maggie's thoughts. In the front of her mind was the extraordinary kiss. It had given her a physical shock, firstly because she hadn't expected it, and secondly because the sensation she had felt as he'd moved his lips back and forth across hers had been so different, so unlike anything else she'd experienced. A shiver of delight had swept over her in the few minutes since the kiss as she'd replayed it in her head. But it had lessened, though, as the minutes ticked by and the kiss had receded into the past.

Now and then she'd stolen a look at his profile; more than anything she wanted to repeat the kiss, to see again what the feeling was that she had experienced. She looked carefully at his eyes to see if she could catch his attention, but he appeared to be concentrating on what was happening on the screen. He reminded her of a small child gripped by an adventure programme.

His lager sat on the ground untouched so Maggie picked it up and began to sip it.

"The cars crash now, see," he suddenly said. Maggie looked at him with embarrassment. What was she doing here with him? She could probably have had a more interesting evening with the horrible Amy. She ought just to get up and go home.

But then there had been the kiss. She sighed and sat back on the settee. Filled with an indefinable frustration, she kept crossing and uncrossing her legs.

Finally, after much bloodletting, the credits of the film rolled. John Cullen took a deep breath and leant back on the seat. He appeared exhausted, as though he had personally taken part in the car chases, the fights, the strutting and posturing across the screen.

"Brilliant," he said, clicking the set off with the remote control. He looked round and seemed momentarily surprised that she was there.

There were a number of reasons why she should have got up and gone home. It was a quarter to ten and his mother would be back soon. He had nothing to say to her and she had nothing to say to him. He was really like a big kid and not even a pair of expensive trainers could change that. She didn't have any feelings for him at all and she was only here so that she'd have something to write and tell Bridget about.

But then there was the kiss.

She closed her eyes and leant towards him. Within

seconds he was there again. Not the little boy who had been watching the film but someone quite different.

He kissed her four, five times before coming up for air, his tongue darting in and out of her mouth, his head twisting from one side to another.

She should have gone home but the feeling in her mouth, her throat, her head held her there. Just one more kiss, she kept saying to herself. As if, like a chocolate from an expensive box, it would be enough to satisfy an appetite somewhere inside her.

It was not enough though.

Her head resting back on the settee she let his mouth send shivers up her back and neck and cautiously pushed her tongue into his mouth. Gaining confidence she put a hand on each side of his face and tried to hold it still while she gently licked his lips. Sometimes the kisses were fast and it was only a split second that his mouth was there and he pulled back; then they were slow and she seemed to be dipping her tongue in and out as though tasting some delicious sundae over and over again.

Food, though, had never given her this buzz in her chest, this aching feeling in her breasts.

He pushed his hand up inside her T-shirt without any warning and she knew it had to stop.

"Wait," she said, but she meant stop. "Wait."

He didn't hear her, or if he did he took no notice.

"No, wait," she said. Somewhere in the back of her head was a growing fear that she couldn't grasp.

"I don't want to do that," she said between mouthfuls of

him, but his head was moving with a frantic air as he tried to slip his hand under her bra, his breath hot on her neck and face.

"Stop," she said. And then she saw, in her head, the marcasite button glittering in her hand and heard the Material Man, his gravelly whisper in her ear. A princess once lost a beautiful diamond, he said moving his fingers back and forth across her flat chest; the prince had to look for it, he said, rubbing small circles over her bony rib-cage; or else he would never marry the princess, he said, his fingers stabbing under her arm.

"No," she finally said, a sick feeling coming into her throat, but John Cullen's hand, finally having eased under her tight bra, was now stuck there. She grabbed his elbow and with a push she expelled him from her.

For a moment he had a shocked expression on his face as though he didn't really know where he was or what he had been doing. He grabbed hold of her wrist and held it tightly. "What's the matter?" he said, panting, his hand now squeezing her wrist so tightly that it was beginning to hurt.

"John, I've got to go," she said quietly and, using her free hand, tried to peel his fingers off her wrist. "John!"

He let her go and she stood up abruptly. Dazed for a second she looked at her wrist and saw a red mark there; it felt as if she'd just had a Chinese burn. Using her fingers she rubbed at it and at the same time found herself gazing at the floor, looking for something.

The marcasite button. She was looking for its glitter but

there was only darkness. She shook her head and looked at John Cullen half lying on the settee, his face expressionless, his mouth opened slightly, his chest lifting up and down as he breathed in and out.

The kisses were nice. The rest she didn't want.

She turned and walked out.

THIRTEEN

"What's Mr Young doing here?" Maggie said. She walked into the kitchen and out through the back door. She could see Long John, his shirt off, his hair tied back in a ponytail, digging furiously in their back garden.

"He's tidying the garden up a bit for me. He charges next to nothing. He's a nice man." Her mum was sitting at the kitchen table, turning over the pages of a newspaper.

"Um," Maggie said without thinking.

"I'm going to plant some shrubs in the corner and Eddie has suggested a rockery on the other side."

"Right," Maggie said. "Does he take photographs, do you know?"

"What do you mean?"

"Like, photography. Is he interested in photography?"

"I don't know."

"Only I thought, when he was in that hospital, he might have taken it up, for therapy, you know."

"I suppose he could have. I don't know. He's never said anything."

"No." Maggie sat back.

So what if the man had a room full of photographs of one girl. It didn't prove a thing. Maybe she should just try and forget about him, act as though she'd never been into his house, never seen the wall covered in pictures.

"Have you heard from Bridget?" her mum said.

"No, I've got to reply to her letter. I'll do it today," she said, knowing that she probably wouldn't. Writing letters was so hard! If only she could speak to her, not on the phone, but face to face for half an hour. Then Bridget could go back to being in Ireland for the next couple of weeks.

What would Bridget have done in her situation? She would have handled the whole thing differently, Maggie knew. Bridget would have made an effort to talk to Long John; she would probably have found out some details about his past by now. Bridget was like that, forward, friendly, whereas she preferred to wait, to hold back.

She sighed. That was probably why Bridget had a boyfriend in Ireland and she had nothing.

Apart from the kissing.

Thinking of it made her smile. Then John Cullen came into her head. She looked at her wrist; there was no mark there even though she fancied she could still feel the burn. His sudden violence had frightened her.

She hadn't meant to lead him on, she hadn't thought. She'd just enjoyed the kissing and hadn't wanted it to stop.

Was it right though? To enjoy someone's kissing even if you didn't like them very much? It had been three days since she had seen him. Amy had said that he'd got a job on one of the stalls down the market while someone was on holiday. It was just as well. He was the last person she wanted to see. The truth was she didn't like him very much at all. The kisses were something different.

And then the marcasite button had sprung into her head; that and the exact words that the Material Man had whispered in her ear. After five years, the fairy story had come out of nowhere into her thoughts. Someone had pressed a button and, like a tape recording, the words had replayed over in her head, just as the Material Man had said them all those years before.

She looked across at her mum.

"I wonder whatever happened to the Material Man?" She said it nervously although the words came out like a casual enquiry, as if she were saying, I wonder whatever happened to the woman next door's cat.

"I mean, what did he do when he moved away? Where do you think he went?"

Her mother's face slipped into its hard look. It was an expression Maggie had not seen since she'd started to balloon up over the past months. Everything about her mum seemed less sharp, less hard, since she'd had a baby growing inside her.

"Do you think he's still got a shop? Do you think he still sells material?"

Her mum stared at her for a moment, as though trying to fathom her out. "I don't know why you even let yourself think of him," she finally said. She stood up from the table and started to move the dishes across to the draining board. She spoke quietly but with menace; Maggie recognized the tone from earlier years when she was being reprimanded in front of other people.

It was used when her mother was trying very hard to control an explosion of rage. "I hope he's in prison now where he deserves to be." She said it calmly, as if she might say, I hope he's very well and living in a nice house.

"Do you think he'd have done it again?"

Her mother took a deep breath. It seemed to take any effort but she spoke softly. "Of course he'd do it again. That type always do. It's a sickness. They couldn't stop even if they wanted to. Most of them don't want to." She leant her back against the sink unit and her face looked tired. "You were too young to understand at the time. You spent months thinking it was your fault. My God! A little girl of ten. As if it could have been your fault." She walked around to where Maggie was sitting and put her hands on her shoulders. Maggie could feel her lump resting on her back.

"I wouldn't mind but he had children of his own. The social workers never even took them away; even after what he'd done to you. It wasn't proved, you see, in a court of law. And that's all that matters." She walked round the table and sat down again. She turned a page of the newspaper as if she was reading but Maggie could see that she was agitated.

After all the times they'd talked about it, she still got upset. Maggie wished she hadn't mentioned it.

Suddenly her mum said, "Has he been around? Have you seen him? Is that why you're asking?"

Maggie looked at her with surprise. "No," she said.

Her mother's mouth was open and her eyes were narrowed. "You've seen him somewhere!"

"No!" Maggie raised her voice. "Of course I haven't. I'd tell you if I had."

Her mother sat looking at her, unsure, her hands joined together in a fist on the table.

"No, honestly. I was just asking. You know, what with Caroline having disappeared, it brought it back into my mind."

Her mother seemed to relax visibly. "Caroline." She looked at the newspaper. "You'd tell me, wouldn't you? If you ever saw him?"

"Yes," Maggie said. She shouldn't have spoken; it was the wrong time to bother her with something like this. She sat in silence except for the thud of earth from Long John's spade.

When the free paper came through the letter box Maggie got it and took it into the front room to read. Caroline's story was all over the front page.

MAN HELD FOR QUESTIONING OVER MISSING GIRL

A 35-year-old father of two is being held for questioning over the disappearance of the missing ten-year-old, Caroline Mitchell. A car, similar to the one owned by the suspect, was sighted at Lordsley Park, about the time of the girl's disappearance. Detectives are reported to have found one of the missing girl's trainers at the disused industrial estate.

Detectives at Leyton Green Police Station say they expect developments shortly.

Ten-year-old Caroline was last seen four weeks ago. A neighbour's son, John Cullen, said he saw her getting into a black car at about 4 o' clock on Monday July 24th. Her mother became worried about her absence at about eight o'clock and notified police.

HOLLOW PONDS FIND

Three weeks ago, after an exhaustive search of the waters around Whipps Cross, divers found a sealed plastic bag which contained items of a child's clothing. These have since been identified as belonging to the missing schoolgirl Lindsey Edwards, not seen now for almost ten years.

The 35-year-old man, currently helping police with their enquiries, was also detained at the time of Lindsey Edwards's disappearance. The police, at the time, were also looking for a second suspect. The man was later released without charge. That case is still open. Full story page four.

Maggie let the newspaper rest on her lap. She was about to open her mouth and tell her mum about the latest developments in the case when she changed her mind. It might start her fretting again. She had only just cheered up after the Material Man discussion.

Instead, she turned to page four to read the full story about Lindsey Edwards, the other missing girl.

MYSTERY OF MISSING SCHOOLGIRL

Lindsey Edwards was last seen on a Wednesday in July ten years ago. She left school at 3.45 and never arrived home. Her parents put an appeal out on TV and her picture was all over the national and local newspapers. Police set up roadblocks all over London and questioned motorists after a young girl of her description was sighted in the back of a car. Two men were in the front.

LOCAL MAN

A couple of days prior to her disappearance, a car with two men was seen cruising around the area near the girl's primary school. A resident took the car's registration number and reported it to the police when the girl disappeared. A local man was picked up by the police for questioning. He denied any knowledge of the missing girl and said that he had had no passenger in his car.

After a search of his home and allotment he was released without charge.

WATERY FIND

Now, ten years later, some of the girl's belongings have been found in the Hollow Ponds. This, plus the fact that another young girl has disappeared, has led to questions about the effectiveness of the police's investigation ten years ago.

The parents of both girls must be asking exactly what it is that the police intend to do to solve these tragic disappearances.

Maggie looked down at the small picture at the side of the article. A young girl's face stared at her and for a moment she thought it was Caroline. It was an old blurred photograph though and looking closer she realized that even though there was something vaguely familiar about it, it wasn't Caroline.

All evening something kept nagging at her. As the credits rolled on programme after programme she felt uneasy, depressed even.

About nine, Amy called across to tell her that she was going away with her mum to her aunt's for a few days and she'd be back soon. Maggie was momentarily touched that she should bother. Perhaps she wasn't so bad after all.

She watched as Amy walked up the street and back towards the flats; her skirt was ridiculously short and she had giant-sized trainers on her feet. Maggie smiled as her bottom waved from side to side. Now that Amy was going away she didn't seem to mind her so much.

She went back to the TV and remembered that she was upset about something. It wasn't about Bridget any more; she'd probably write to her the next day. She wasn't feeling down about John Cullen; she wouldn't see much more of him this holiday and she could always ignore him in school.

It could have been her mum's reaction to the Material

Man; every now and then she looked across at her and fancied she could see a nervous tic working at the side of her mouth, a protective clutching of her lump. It couldn't just be that, though; there was something irking her and she couldn't work out what it was.

It was just after the late evening news that it came to her.

"Where's the newspaper?" she demanded. Her mum and dad looked sleepily at her.

"Which one?" her mum said, her lip still curling slightly as though Maggie had just asked another question about the Material Man.

"The free one. The free one."

"In the kitchen bin." She heard her mum mumble on after the door shut behind her. Putting her hand into the murky blackness of the bin, her face visibly crumpling at the smell that threw itself at her, she rescued the wrinkled, slightly damp pages of the paper.

She pulled it open so that page four lay on the floor in front of her.

She looked at the picture of the girl who had been missing for ten years.

It was tiny and blurred and it didn't look anything like Caroline.

She'd seen it before, though. She'd seen it in various sizes and in absolute detail.

She'd seen it plastered all over Long John's white wall.

FOURTEEN

The next morning Maggie cut both articles from the newspaper and put them inside plastic covers that she had in an old ring binder.

She read them over two or three more times and looked at the small blurred picture of Lindsey Edwards. She thought about the pictures on Long John's wall. The same photo over and over again; sometimes bigger, sometimes smaller.

Her mum came into her room.

"Here," she said, and threw a letter on to her bed. Maggie picked it up. It had a "Waterford" postmark and on the front was Bridget's neat handwriting. Another letter and she hadn't even replied to the last one.

It was probably all about Bridget and Brendan.

She could have written to Bridget about her date with John Cullen but she hadn't had the heart. She sighed and put Bridget's unopened letter on her bedside cabinet. She had more important things to think about.

She should go to the police. At the very least she should tell her dad. She picked up the plastic folders with the newspaper articles in and held them.

But what did it all prove?

What if she told her dad and they went into Long John's and all the photos were gone? She had no proof.

Proof of what?

She lay back on her bed and let the articles drop out of her hand. She closed her eyes and let the facts swim about inside her head.

Caroline Mitchell missing; Long John at the Hollow Ponds; Lindsey Edwards disappeared ten years ago; photographs of Lindsey Edwards on the wall; two men sighted in a car; crying in the night; clothes found at Hollow Ponds; child's belongings found in Long John's; a girl's plait of hair; police looking for a second suspect; Long John in a mental hospital for ten years; "Man held for questioning by police".

It was all a muddle. If it were written down on a piece of paper it would probably be like a sprawling chart with arrows and circles pointing here and there, linking some facts and not others. It wouldn't be in a nice clean list.

Maggie sat up.

She could organize it into a list. She could write each point out neatly and clearly, as she did sometimes in school. "Make a list of all the facts then put them into order of importance".

She tore some paper out of a pad and sat at a small table.

If she organized it into simple points she might see some connections, some link. Then she would have something she could tell her dad.

Some time later she sat in front of a piece of paper with the list on it. It was neatly written and at first glance might have looked like a piece of schoolwork.

Now she had to choose what she thought was the most

important fact to put at the top of her second list.

She chose "Photographs of Lindsey Edwards on long John's wall".

Next she wrote, "Lindsey Edwards missing ten years ago".

Then, "Long John in mental hospital for ten years".

Underneath she put, "Caroline Mitchell disappears after Long John leaves hospital".

She began to feel excited. With just these four things, there seemed to be some link. She took her ruler and underlined them all. After each one she added an oversized exclamation mark.

Then she was stuck.

The other facts all seemed to be vague and none seemed to stick out as being more important than any others. Some of them didn't make any sense at all. She read over the newspaper articles again. Her eyes focused on the headline.

"Man held for questioning by police".

The police were questioning a thirty-five-year-old man about Caroline's disappearance. He was the same man they had questioned ten years ago about Lindsey Edwards's abduction. A resident had seen his car cruising the streets near Lindsey's school and he or she had taken the registration number. When Lindsey disappeared they'd rung the police. TWO men had been seen in the car but the police had only questioned him.

Now, ten years later, they had taken him in for questioning again. His car had been sighted down at

Lousy Park. He was married and had two kids but the police still thought he might be the man.

If the police were right and he was the guilty man then it made a nonsense of her list and her thoughts about Long John.

She looked over the list again. She read the newspaper article. There was some link, there had to be. A grown man doesn't have photographs of a young dead girl in his room without a good reason.

Her eyes focused on the last but one fact she had written on her list. She held her breath for a moment and then in large letters she wrote the words TWO MEN across the bottom of the page.

There had been TWO MEN in the car when Lindsey Edwards went missing. TWO MEN. The police had ONE of them in custody. What had happened to the other?

Had he had a nervous breakdown? Gone into a mental hospital?

Was Long John the second man? Was that the link?

An hour or so later Maggie started to write it all down, as though it was a story. At the top of it she wrote, *Dear Bridget, What do you make of all this?*

It took a while and she used three sheets of A4 paper. She explained what she knew and then what she thought had happened.

As she wrote the words down the whole story seemed to take a firmer shape. What had been unclear before now seemed obvious.

Long John and another man had abducted and killed Lindsey. They'd put most of her clothes and belongings in a black plastic bag and thrown them in one of the ponds. (Long John had kept some of her things.)

The man whose car it was had been arrested but not charged.

Long John had had a breakdown and spent years in a mental hospital.

When he'd been released he had come back to the area where it had happened and been involved in the same thing again. They always do it again, her mother had said.

The same man was being held for questioning, but the police had never caught up with the SECOND man, Long John.

At the end of her letter she wrote, *After I post this letter, I'm going to tell my dad.*

She put the sheets of paper on her bedside table and lay back on her bed. She felt better, her head clearer, now that she had made the decision, now that she knew what she was going to do.

FIFTEEN

Maggie shoved the letter she had written into an envelope and went out on to the landing to see what the commotion was all about.

Looking down the stairs, she could see her mum seated on the bottom stair, her upper body leaning sideways against the banister. Her dad was opening and closing drawers in the kitchen.

"What's wrong?" Maggie said, but she didn't need an answer. Her mum's hand gripped one of the brown banisters and held it tightly for a few seconds. Although Maggie couldn't see her face she could see the back of her neck and her shoulders and for a few seconds they were held rigid as though they were made of stone. Then she relaxed and her whole back seemed to sink into the gaps between the banisters.

"What's wrong?" Maggie said needlessly. Her dad was walking along the hallway from the kitchen. In his hand was her mum's zip-up bag full of the things that she would need to have a baby. It was an old sports bag and in it her mum had carried trainers, shorts, T-shirts, towels, deodorant. Now she was carrying different things; nighties, underwear, slippers, a babygro, disposable nappies.

"Is it time to go to the hospital?" she said, and a feeling

of fear started to niggle away at her stomach. Her mum had never been away from her before. For a moment she saw her, shrunken in height, ludicrously wide round the middle, walking to and fro in a sanitized, impersonal room surrounded by sharp, thin women in starched hats. It was a silly image; hospitals weren't like that. Even so, she found herself looking at the sports bag sitting at the foot of the stairs, and feeling a sense of dread.

"Do you want me to come?" she said, walking down the stairs, her feet feeling like bricks on every step.

"No love," her dad said, standing protectively above the bag. He was opening his wallet and checking inside it.

She finally came alongside her mum, whose face she was expecting to look drained, waxen, strained. Instead, her cheeks were rosy and she gave a weak smile.

"Don't worry," her mum said, "it doesn't hurt all the time. Remember I told you about the contractions. There won't be any more for a while."

"I'll come to the hospital," Maggie said, her mind empty now of Long John or Caroline or Lindsey Edwards.

"Relax. Relax," her dad said in a quiet and calm voice. In his hand was a five-pound note. "I've not got any smaller. Get yourself a takeaway and I'll ring as soon as I know what's happening."

"I'd rather come," Maggie said, the five-pound note limp in her fingers. But her dad had taken his car keys from the hook on the wall and was opening the front door. Her mum stood up and linked her arm through Maggie's.

"Listen," she said, "this is Dad's big moment. I've been educating him for months for this. He wasn't there when you were born. Too squeamish, he said. I want him with me this time. You know that." Her mum was smiling but her steps were unsteady and her bulk seemed to weigh her to one side. She seemed much shorter and Maggie could see the top of her head, the way her hair hadn't been combed, the strands of grey among the brown.

Her dad was ahead, opening the car door and putting the sports bag in the back seat.

More than anything Maggie wanted to go with them, to sit curled up in the back seat of the car, in between them as she had always done. She wanted to be there as her mum lumbered up the steps of the hospital. She wanted to check out her bed, to unpack her things and tidy them away in the bedside cabinet. It wouldn't take her a minute to go and get her brush and her hairdryer and take them with her to the hospital; she could style her mum's hair as she sat waiting for the baby to come. She could stop when the contractions came.

"Come on, love." Her dad was at the gate. Maggie wanted to hold on to her mother's arm; she would be a help in the hospital. She could run down to the shop to get cans of Coke or magazines.

"I could stay outside the delivery room," she said, her voice cracking.

"Hey." Her mum squeezed her. "Dad wants to be in charge now. We can let him, can't we, just this once. When I get home, that's when I'm going to need you. He'll be no good at all then." She kissed Maggie on the cheek.

"I'll ring you as soon as I know what's happening," her dad shouted as he helped her mum into the passenger seat. The door closed softly and Maggie watched him as he rounded the car and got into the driver's seat. He waved maniacally at her, as if she was half a mile away instead of a few feet. "Bye, love."

As they drove away, up the street, she felt something in her hand. She looked down. It was the five-pound note.

The car was almost at the corner. When it was out of sight she slumped against the side of the porch, feeling weary, as though she had just had a great contraction.

It was then that she noticed Long John walking down the street towards her. A niggle of fear played around in her stomach. She stepped back into the hallway and closed the front door.

SIXTEEN

It was eight o'clock and she stood at the upstairs back-room window and watched Long John in his garden. It was getting dark and she was feeling hungry. She could go along to the chip shop or ring up for a pizza; both of these took effort, though, and since her mum had gone she felt drained.

Long John was digging a hole. It was round and it was deep, judging by the pile of earth that was building up beside him.

The fear Maggie had felt when she saw him earlier had dissipated. She was watching Long John in a detached way as though he was a gardener on a TV programme. Beside him on the ground was a small tree or a bush. The bottom of it was wrapped in plastic, as though he'd just bought it from a garden centre. His tools were scattered round as well and by the back door she could see a pale wooden box covered by what looked like a tea towel.

Perhaps she was adding two and two up and getting minus five.

There was no real evidence that Long John was the second man. Maybe there was no second man. People make mistakes. The man the police had in custody probably worked on his own. "Worked"! It sounded like a job; something someone did for a living, stealing young girls away.

She sat down on the floor and leant her head back against the wall. The room she was in used to be a spare room. Now it was the room her mum and dad had got ready for the new baby. She still called it "the back room"; her mum called it "the nursery".

It was painted white and half way up the wall was a border with a brightly coloured balloon design on it. Over in the corner was a wooden cot with a bird mobile hanging above it. Maggie smiled for a moment. What would a baby think if it looked up and saw half a dozen flamboyantly coloured birds whizzing round above its head? She thought of her mum. What was she doing right at that very moment?

In the other alcove was a chest of drawers that her mum and dad had bought and stripped of paint some months before. She walked over and casually opened the top drawer. In it were cellophane packets of babygros and tiny pairs of socks; there were packets of baby wipes and large, soft, cloud-like packets of cotton wool.

In the corner of the drawer was a white glossy book. The words "Baby's First Book" were embossed in gold italics on the front. Maggie picked it up and went back over to the window. She glanced down at Long John, who was taking a rest from digging. He was standing with his back to her and drinking from a can. It was cloudy and looked to be almost dark, even though it was still early. Maggie could only make out the shape of the pile of earth on the ground and she could only dimly see the hole that the tree was going to go into. It was a funny time of day to plant a tree.

The wooden box had been moved from his back door closer to the hole. It stood out in the greying night like a small rectangle of light. Something was hanging over its side and Maggie couldn't make out what it was.

She sat on the chair by the window. It was really too dark for her to read the words in the book but she couldn't be bothered to go over and turn the light switch on. From behind her she could hear the slowed-down notes of the mobile.

She turned the first page. Date of Birth; Time of Birth; Hospital; Weight; Length. It was all blank, waiting to be filled in. She flicked a few pages: Date of First Smile; Date of First Word; Date of First Step. Who was supposed to fill it in, she wondered. Her mum? Her dad? She flicked over a few more pages: Baby's First Lock of Hair. She turned the page but stopped and turned back. She read it over again. After sitting very still for a moment she stood up and in the darkening night saw that Long John had gone inside for a moment and the white box was there on the ground, near to the hole, but in clear view.

She dropped the book and raced downstairs and into the garden. She leant over the fence, looking at the box. It was only feet away and in the deepening night she could see a tea towel was covering most of the things in it. One corner of the tea towel was ruffled, though, and peeping out from beneath it, like the tail of animal, was the thick brown plait of hair.

She held her breath for a moment and looked at the few inches of it that she could see, curling over the edge of the box, making a "J" shape. There was a rattle from inside Long John's back door and she ran quickly back into her house.

She went back into the spare room and stood by the window, watching to see what was going to happen. There was no sign of Long John for at least another ten minutes.

It was almost completely dark by the time he came into the garden again. She couldn't make him out clearly but she could see his shape moving around the garden. He bent over from time to time and she guessed he was picking up tools or just tidying. He'd changed his clothes, or at least put a dark sweater on. Apart from his face, his body merged completely into the dark.

He stood for a while facing the hole and then began to move. It was completely dark by that time but she could just make out what he was doing. He squatted down by the wooden box and placed what looked like a lid on the top of it. Then, using both hands, he picked it up. He slowly walked across to the hole he'd dug and, kneeling down, placed the box into the hole. He stood back for a few moments and then, taking a spade, he threw a few shovelfuls of dirt into it.

Maggie stood clutching the side curtain while he did this. Her mind was blank and the muscles in her calves and shoulders felt like iron. Eventually, after what seemed like hours, he stopped and went across to the tree. He stood for a moment and then suddenly turned round to look at her window. She ducked and stood with her back to the wall. After about thirty seconds she turned and carefully looked back towards him. He was staring across at some of the other houses.

It was then that she saw that he hadn't just changed his sweater, he'd put a shirt on and a tie. In fact it looked as though he was wearing a suit.

He took the tree and walked across to the hole. She couldn't see what he was doing and he was bent down a lot. After a few minutes he walked backwards and she guessed he'd planted it.

In less than a minute he was gone. The garden was empty apart from the discarded tea towel.

For some reason she knew he wasn't coming back. She rushed out of the spare room and along to her mum and dad's bedroom and pulled the curtain aside. His front door was just slamming and she watched him go up his path and get into his car. After a few seconds he drove away.

Maggie sat on her bed in her dressing gown with her feet out of the duvet. It was twelve thirty. Her dad was due back any minute. Her mum's contractions had stopped at about ten o'clock. They were keeping her in anyway and were going to start her off again in the morning. Her dad was coming home and would go back to the hospital early. He'd told her on the phone not to wait up.

She had waited up, though.

She had to tell him about Long John; she had to tell

him about the pictures of Lindsey Edwards – missing for ten years – that covered one wall of his room; about the purse covered in beads, the child's toy animal, the underwear that she had found in the drawer of his desk, the plait of child's hair.

All these things that he had buried beneath a tree in the garden that evening.

She looked at her bedside table. The letter that she had written to Bridget was still there. She had forgotten to post it. She screwed it up in her hand and threw it towards the bin.

When her dad came in she was going to tell him everything.

When she woke up her light was out. She looked at her clock; it was 3.48. She was still in her dressing gown although her dad had covered her with the duvet. She got up out of bed and tiptoed to the next bedroom.

He was lying flat on his face, fully dressed. The only things he had taken off were his shoes.

He was sound asleep. Exhaustion must have overtaken him when he'd got back from the hospital.

It didn't really matter. She'd get up early in the morning and talk to him then. She got back into bed and set her clock for six thirty.

The front door slamming woke her before six thirty. It was 5.45. She ran into her dad's bedroom only to hear the engine of the car starting up. On her mum's dressing table was a note:

Didn't want to wake you. Had to be at the hospital by six. I'll ring you as soon as anything of note happens. Get yourself some lunch with this. Love Dad xxxxxxxx

Underneath was another five-pound note. Maggie held it in her hand and felt like crying.

SEVENTEEN

Her dad phoned at about half eleven and said that the doctors had put her mum on "the drip". He said he didn't know when it would all start happening and he had no idea whether he'd be home early or late or not at all. Could she cope? he asked. Wouldn't she rather go over to her aunt's house in Ilford?

Maggie's voice was calm on the phone, even though her finger was tracing frantic doodles on the wall. She said that being on her own was no problem, why should it be? Now and then, though, she pulled the phone wire to its maximum length and stretched her neck so that she could see if anyone was in Long John's back garden. She said goodbye confidently but replaced the receiver clumsily and it clattered off and banged against the wall as it hung on its flex. She tensed her shoulders and looked around guiltily as she lifted it back on to the wall phone.

The doctors had put her mum "on the drip".

She was lying there, a tiny tube going into her arm. Her contractions had probably stopped and the doctors were trying to get her going again.

She walked up and down the hallway of her house for a while trying to visualize what was happening in the hospital. Her mum lying in bed, her dad walking up and down, or sitting rubbing her back or helping her to breathe properly.

Now and then the sound of a door closing from next door made her stop and put her ear flat on to the adjoining wall. Once she thought she heard a harsh, desperate laugh, but when she stood still she heard it moving away, along the street.

It didn't matter that it hadn't been him laughing; the fact was he was only feet away, through six inches of brick and plaster.

And her mum and dad were a mile and a half away, in a labour ward in Whipps Cross Hospital.

She should have told her dad. There was no doubt in her mind about that. Maybe as far back as when she first saw the pictures and the plait of hair. If only she hadn't been showing off to Amy and John, she might have taken it a bit more seriously herself.

How could she tell him now, with her mum about to give birth?

She pictured Long John leaving his house the previous evening, dressed up in a suit, looking as though he was going somewhere special.

What if he was going to find someone else? Her mum had said that; they always do it again, they never change.

Was the Material Man doing it again somewhere? Was there some little shop full of lace and cottons and patterns and scissors in which he sat and waited for a young girl?

Maggie suddenly felt a great sadness inside her. She stopped pacing up and down and leant against the wall.

She had only wanted to look at the button, sparkling like a diamond, on his waistcoat. She hadn't even minded listening to his strange story about the princess who'd lost the jewel in among her clothes. Maggie liked grown-ups; grown-ups liked Maggie. He was a strange little fat man who couldn't breathe very well and as well as being polite she had felt sorry for him, always seated in the little wooden chair behind the counter, among the dust and cobwebs; he'd seemed trapped there, never seeing the outside world. She hadn't minded being nice to him.

She pursed her lips together and felt herself starting to cry.

What was happening to her? It had been five years since it all happened.

Maggie had run home after getting out of his shop, her pace slowing as she got nearer to her street. She stood at the corner and felt her heart galloping ahead of her. She inhaled breath after breath and felt as though she'd just run a race. Calmer, she walked into her house and sat down. The Material Man hadn't had any of those little strawberry-shaped buttons. He might have some in next week.

On the table there were two banana sandwiches and a packet of chocolate fingers. Her mum was ironing and singing along with a song on the radio. Once or twice she held the iron as though it were a microphone. Maggie laughed and took bites from round the edge of her sandwich. She left the chocolate fingers. She spent part of the lunch time sitting on the toilet.

She had a tummy upset, she said.

Bridget called for her to go back to school. Walking up the high road, she told her about going into the shop. Only don't tell anyone, she said. She described the waistcoat; the button, the story, the man's hands. Only promise you won't say anything to anyone, she said. She even remembered the Material Man's hot breath on her ear and him getting up out of his chair to come after her. Only, if you say anything, my mum'll go mad, she'll tell me off, she said.

That night, watching the telly, there was a knock on the door. Maggie got up to answer it. It was Bridget's mum. I'm after your mother, she'd said, and Maggie knew then that Bridget had told.

She went up and sat on the toilet while Bridget's mum had gone into the back kitchen with her mum. She couldn't hear their voices, only the sounds of the TV. After what seemed like a long time the front door slammed.

She sat there on the toilet seat, even though she'd long finished, her insides felt tangled up with apprehension. Something bad had happened in the material shop and it was probably her fault. Her mum and dad knew about it by now.

Eventually, she pulled the flush and went out. There, at the bottom of the stairs, were her mum and dad. They started to come up towards her.

"I'm sorry," she said, her voice cracking up, "I'm sorry, I didn't mean to." But she couldn't go on because her dad had picked her up and hugged her tightly. She buried her head in his shoulder and in the darkness there she could feel her mum's hand stroking her head and rubbing her neck.

In five years she'd hardly thought about it. And now it was haunting her. She sat on the bottom stair and her chest felt sore with the aggravation of it all. Her skin was wet and she used her knuckles to wipe away the tears.

She looked at her watch and cleared her throat a couple of times.

Five minutes later she looked at it again.

Nothing had changed except that she had cried herself dry. Her mum was still in hospital. Long John was still next door. The plait of hair and the other things were buried under a tree in his garden. The Material Man had still sat her on his knee as if she had been his little girl; as if he had been her dad. Without asking her, he had touched her skin; his fingers, like burglars, breaking into her clothes; trying to steal something from her. Nothing could change that.

Sitting crying on the stairs couldn't change anything.

She got up and went to the bathroom. Filling the sink with water, she dipped her face into it. She took a handful of water and splashed it over her forehead and the front of her hair.

She couldn't involve her dad now, but she could tell the police.

It meant getting hold of the evidence that Long John

had buried. The tree would have to be dug up, the hair and the other things taken out.

She would have to dig it up in the middle of the night. She looked at herself in the mirror above the washbasin.

It would be pitch dark. It would be hard work. She couldn't do it on her own.

She needed someone to help her.

It was Thursday so the market was packed full of shoppers. Amy had said that John was working on a fruit and veg stall near Woolworths. Maggie counted eight fruit and veg stalls within fifty feet either way. There was no sign of John Cullen.

She bought a packet of chips and a drink and leant against the wall waiting for him to show up. The chips were in a cardboard packet the shape of an ice-cream cone. It meant that the vinegar ran to the bottom and dribbled on to her hand. Either that or it dripped on to her clothes. In the end she held it away from her like a bunch of flowers and reached across for the chips. Her drink she placed on a ledge behind her.

After about twenty minutes he came along. He was in the process of taking a lolly out of its paper. After a short struggle to open the wrapper he took a deep breath and blew hard into it. As the paper peeled off, Maggie could see that the lolly was in the shape of a foot.

He saw her at once although his face didn't register anything. When he came walking towards her she felt embarrassment growing. It was the first time she had seen him since the date. Involuntarily she grasped the wrist that he had hurt. Would he help her now? After what had happened?

"All right?" he said when he came closer. She looked him straight in the face and at the same time put her hand up the back of her T-shirt and pulled her bra down.

"What time do you finish?" she said, her voice shaking. He had most of the toes of the lolly in his mouth and for a moment she thought that he probably didn't even remember the other night.

"Time we finished clearing away. About eight, I suppose." Around his lips was a thin line of maroon colouring from the lolly.

"I need you to help me with something. Will you come over to me after work?"

"What's happened?" he said.

"Come round tonight and I'll tell you," she said, and picking her can of drink up from the ledge she walked away.

EIGHTEEN

"Here, take this shovel," Maggie hissed. "You dig and I'll watch. When you're tired, I'll dig and you watch. That way there's no chance of him coming out and catching us." As she said this, Maggie stared intently at Long John's back door. It was slightly ajar as it always was and from inside it she could see his hall light, a greyish yellow.

"Hold this, then." John Cullen handed her a sherbet fountain, half empty, the yellow paper round the top wet where he had been tipping it back straight into his mouth.

"Try to dig it out without injuring the tree," she whispered, holding it at arm's length, as though it were a dirty hanky.

"Yes, yes," he said tersely. He was digging with a small hand shovel, it was all she could find; it would take some time. She looked at her watch and tutted. It was too dark to make out the time.

It was probably about quarter past eleven.

John Cullen had arrived about nine and she had blustered through her story. He had listened, although from time to time he'd looked preoccupied, as though he wasn't with her at all. As though his head was focusing on some other story entirely. "Are you listening?" she'd said once or twice, particularly when she'd got to bits that she thought were significant – the photos on the wall or the burying of the plait. "I'm with you," he'd said. "I'm with you." And, not for the first time, she'd wondered whether he really was "with them" in any serious way.

Then her dad phoned. He'd said that all was well and that her mum was "seven centimetres". Maggie had said great, well done, as though her dad had had something to do with it. Afterwards she'd screwed her nose and mouth up and thought of the pain her mum was probably in.

"My mum's cervix is seven centimetres," she'd said to John Cullen when he'd asked. She'd said it with a half-smile, sure that he wouldn't know what she was talking about. He'd nodded sagely though. She'd not been able to resist saying, "You don't even know what that is!"

He'd taken a deep breath and said, "When a woman gives birth, the cervix – the neck of the womb – opens during contractions. It has to open to ten centimetres before the woman is ready to go into second-stage labour."

He said it confidently and in one go – almost as though he'd learned it off by heart.

"How do you know?" She'd said it aggressively. John Cullen was like two different boys. The big mawkish kid who didn't care what he looked like, who sucked lollies in public and hung around with his kid sister; then there was this adult John who liked long, panting kisses and knew about women's gynaecological details.

"When shall we start digging?" he'd answered, and turned away. That was another thing about him. Every now and then a little door seemed to close on his face. Just when she thought she was getting somewhere, finding out about him, his eyes glazed over and his lips closed as though they were lined with Velcro.

"We'll have to wait until he goes to bed." Even as she said it, though, she knew it wouldn't do. Long John stayed up until all hours; hadn't she been the one who had heard him crying at three o'clock in the morning? She had no idea when her dad would be home, but she was sure he wouldn't be away all night.

John, on the other hand, could come and go as he pleased. His mum and sister had gone away for a few days. No one would miss him.

About eleven, Maggie went into the back garden to look for signs of life from Long John's house. The kitchen light was off but there was light from further in the house, up near the front.

"He's probably watching the telly. We'll have to take a chance," she said.

It was risky, digging up Long John's back garden while he was sitting watching the TV thirty or forty feet away. It was a gamble they would have to take. Any other night and her dad would be home. Soon after that her mum would be home with a new baby. It had to be done now.

Although it was dark in the garden Maggie could, after a few minutes, see the outline of the fence, the bushes, the plastic chair that Long John sat in sometimes.

"I'll have to dig round the tree. And then pull it up by its main stem," John Cullen whispered.

"Ssh," she said, her eyes darting round. There were also the neighbours on the other side to consider. What if one of them looked out of the window?

She watched John Cullen dig. He was kneeling on the ground and scooping out earth. The line he had dug looked like a moat that surrounded the small tree. He reminded her of a child on a beach making an elaborate sand castle. All he needed was a plastic pot in which to make mud pies.

She looked back towards the house. Inside it was a mentally sick man. It was nearly midnight and she was in his garden making holes like a gravedigger.

John Cullen was making grunting sounds.

"Shall I take over?" she whispered. He'd stopped for a moment and was taking deep breaths. He nodded and sat cross-legged on the ground.

She gave him the sherbet fountain back and got on to her knees. She dug hard into the ground, taking great shovelfuls of earth, three, four, five, six times. The seventh time she hit a solid object. She was about to open her mouth and say something when she suddenly felt John Cullen crashing on top of her and an urgent whisper of "SSH . . . SSH" in her ear.

The light from the kitchen window and door abruptly lit the garden up. It stretched out from the house in great yellow parallelograms. Peeking out from beneath John Cullen, Maggie could see that one of the shapes seemed to be pointing in their direction and the illumination it gave ended only an arm's length from where she lay. The side of her face was on the ground and her arms and legs felt rigid; her back was tense, holding the weight of John

Cullen, who was pinning her down. To throw him off meant noise and movement. He probably knew that too; that's why he wasn't moving.

The silence of the garden was broken by sounds from the kitchen. Maggie heard a tap being turned on and off; a cup being placed on a surface; the new fridge door opening and shutting. Closing her eyes, she saw Long John standing in the tiny room, waiting for the kettle to boil, his eyes sleepy, his ponytail gone, his hair in lank strands.

For a few moments she heard nothing.

Then a great thumping sound came into her ear from across the garden. As though someone further away was slowly playing a drum. All the time she could feel John Cullen lying across her back, his face over her shoulder, an inch away from hers.

The beating sound seemed to get louder but it wasn't coming from across the garden. It was coming from inside her ribcage. For a moment or so she tried to hold herself more rigidly, in the hope that it would quieten. Like a fist, it continued to hit at her chest, more insistent each time, like someone throwing themselves at a door, harder and harder, pushing until it burst open.

The clinking sound of a spoon against a cup and the opening and closing of cupboard doors broke the crescendo in her lungs and her heart seemed to shrink, its sound getting lower on each beat. Long John was finishing. He would turn the light out and go back into the front room. They would not be discovered.

Her relief was so great that she didn't mind the feel of the dirt on her face and the tickle of grass around her ears. She didn't even mind the thought of the insects that might be shuffling around there in the dark: centipedes that moved like a chorus of dancers, sluggish earwigs, manic ants.

The sound of receding footsteps was followed by the click of the light going off. Maggie's whole frame relaxed. John Cullen rolled sideways and lay with his back on the ground. Unable to speak, Maggie sat up, leaning on her elbow, her face off the ground, away from the teeming insect life that she was sure was there.

She was about to say, "That was close", or "let's get out of here", when John Cullen moved quickly towards her and began to kiss her hard on the mouth.

Even the tension of the previous few minutes couldn't stop the feeling that shot through her stomach like an electric current. It wasn't the right time and it certainly wasn't the right place. All the same she didn't stop him. Just one, she said to herself, just one kiss.

The trouble was that after a few minutes the kisses weren't enough. She felt John Cullen's hands moving towards her breasts. It was up to her to stop him, to say that she wanted to get on with things. But she didn't. She didn't want to stop him. Her eyes closed and she lay back on the grass and for a few minutes the hole in the ground and the missing girl went completely out of her mind.

Amid the kissing she could hear something. A whisper in her ear; some indefinable sentences, breathy words that she couldn't identify. John Cullen had rolled on top of her and was pulling at the waistband of her jeans.

"What?" she said hoarsely. And he repeated some broken words in her ear, as though he was having trouble finding the breath to say them all in one go.

But then the words turned into a story she knew. A princess lived in a beautiful castle. A prince from another land was in love with her. Was John Cullen saying these words? She didn't know; she didn't think so.

The prince had given the princess the most beautiful diamond that there ever was. She had treasured it and wore it on a fine gold chain around her neck. One day the chain snapped and the diamond fell in among her clothes. The prince had to look for it. He looked up under her sleeves, in the folds of her skirt, in among the intricate lace of her collar. He couldn't find it anywhere.

Maggie had forgotten that she was in Long John's garden. The soft earth was like a bed and she let her head lie back among the patchy grass. The prince continued his search. He put his hand down the front of her dress and searched among her underclothes. He lifted her layers of petticoats but there was still no diamond.

At the end of a long kiss Maggie could hear the sound of her jeans being unzipped. She opened her eyes and saw John Cullen's face deep in concentration, trying to pull at the waist of her jeans. Over to the side she saw something yellow on the ground. It was the empty sherbet fountain packet lying discarded. She looked back at John Cullen and felt revulsion. The story in her head had stopped.

She became aware again of where she was. It was pitch dark and she was lying in Long John's garden with a half-dug hole beside her.

"For God's sake," she said trying to sit up, to pull away from underneath him. "This isn't the time!"

She doubted in that moment whether there ever would be a time with John Cullen, no matter how exhilarating the kisses were.

"We've got to get the evidence dug up!" she said, raising her knees to put a barrier between them. "Come on! We can do that any time." It was a lie and she knew it as she spoke. It seemed to move him though.

She took the shovel as he held the stem of the tree. She wedged it against the side of what felt like the wooden box. It was too heavy to move. She'd have to dig down to it. John Cullen pulled at the tree as she edged the shovel round its roots. After a minute or so it began to loosen and with a few more shovelfuls behind her it finally dislodged from the ground.

Underneath it was a beige wooden box. It was an oblong, about the size of a toolbox.

"What's in that?" John Cullen said, his voice – for once – apprehensive.

"Just the stuff I found in his house, I expect, the toys, the photos, the hair," she said, but there was unease in her voice. For the first time she wondered whether there might be something else, something more macabre, inside the casket.

"Help me with it," she said, and the two of them leant

into the tiny hole and got a hand under each corner. "When I count three, pick it up. One two three."

It was sitting on the grass between them and neither of them spoke.

"We can't carry that over the fence," John Cullen said.

"It's not nailed down, look. We can just open it and take out what we want."

But neither of them moved. They looked at each other and then at the box. A screech of brakes in the distance shook them and Maggie finally knelt down and, taking a deep breath, pushed the lid of the box off.

The box was full up to the top. Maggie couldn't make out all the things in it.

"Look," she said. She held up the plait of hair and showed it to John Cullen. He backed away from her. His face had a shocked look on it. It was as if she was holding up a severed limb, not a length of dead hair.

"It's all right," she said, "it's just got the things in that I told you."

But he was still taking backward strides. In the dark she couldn't quite make out his expression but he seemed transfixed.

"Oh for God's sake," she said. Her voice was normal, as though it were the middle of the day and she were standing chatting in the street.

John Cullen turned suddenly and in a deft movement jumped over the fence and started to run up her garden.

"John!" she said indignantly, turning to watch him run into the back door of her own house. There was a movement behind her and she stopped in her tracks.

She turned round and felt her stomach fall down to her bowels.

A couple of feet away, standing silently in the dark, was long John.

NINETEEN

Maggie was sitting in a chair by the side of the desk in Long John's back room. She was still holding the plait of hair, as if in her fright it had become fused to her hand, like a rope that she was clinging on to.

"Do you want a cup of tea?" he said. He was sitting on another chair a foot or so away. She tensed at his words, as though he had just said, "Do you want to come and sit on my knee?"

Looking to her side she saw that all the photographs of Lindsey Edwards had gone.

She shook her head slowly, her lips closed tightly as though stuck together. Her neck and shoulders felt rigid although she was sitting lightly on the chair, ready, she thought, at a moment's notice to leap off it and run away.

"Was that the boy from the flats?" he said, looking straight at her, his eyes penetrating her rigid stance.

She ignored him and looked away. She needed a weapon of some sort; something she could use when he turned against her.

"Why were you stealing from me?" he said, leaning towards her. He appeared to have lost his sluggish speech. There was none of the previous hesitation in his voice. She continued to look at him. Close up he seemed much smaller; in the dark of the garden he had looked about seven feet tall. His face was thin and he had bright blue eyes that were surrounded by deep lines; laughter lines, she had heard them called, but he wasn't laughing.

She gripped the hair tightly, as though it were an iron bar and she was about to swing it at his head.

It felt limp in her hand. She looked down at it and then quickly back to Long John. His eyes broke away from her face and he stared at the hair. Even though he'd already seen it in her hand in the garden he gave a low gasp and his face crumpled; the lines around his eyes deepened and his forehead seemed to fold in on itself. He looked like an old man.

Maggie felt an advantage. Maybe the plait of hair was just as much a weapon as any solid object.

"You thought you'd got rid of this," she said, her voice croaky, her knees shaking with fear. "You thought no one knew about this and the toys and the pictures." She stopped for a minute as Long John stood up, his arms swinging as though he had no control over them. She held her breath waiting for him to grab her or hit her. But he didn't and she sat, like a statue, watching him as he walked across to the other wall and, holding his palms flat, leant against the plaster.

He stood there for a few moments, his hand pushing against the wall, his feet splayed, looking like a suspect who was waiting to be searched. It was as if he'd forgotten her.

She stood up and began to edge along the wall at her back. He was moaning and she moved her feet slowly, taking care to make no noise. She was a stride away from the door when he turned towards her.

"You thought," she said, her words hesitant as though she was afraid of what she might say next, "that no one knew about Lindsey Edwards."

He flinched at the sound of the girl's name, as though it were a sharp object that she had just thrown at him.

"Give me the hair," he said.

"That's for the police, they know I'm here," she added quickly. "John will have told them by now. They'll be on their way."

"Give me the hair," he said, moving towards her. She stepped sideways and her fingers were touching the door knob. He held his hand out; he was going to try and stop her.

She turned the knob anyway. What could he do to her? The handle turned but the door did not click open as she'd hoped. She remembered the spoke that stuck out on the other side.

"Give me the hair," he said, his voice steadier now; he had the advantage, he knew that. He could tell she was afraid. Was this what happened with the girls he stole away? Did he wait until they were collapsing with fright before he attacked them?

"The police will be here any minute. If you hurt me. . ."

"Give me the hair!" he said, and stepped towards her.

This was it. He was going to hurt her. Without thinking, she stepped back against the door and swung the plait up in the air, towards his face. He ducked back but it caught him on the side.

She knew it wouldn't hurt him. She had hoped it would frighten him. Instead it sent him into a rage.

He grabbed her arm and tried to prise her fingers open. With her free hand she started to pound at the back of his head. "Give it to me," he said, blinking his eyes with each hit. "Give it to me," he repeated, pulling her fingers back, one by one, off the hair. "GIVE IT TO ME!" he screamed and the shock of his voice made her drop the hair on to the floor. In a second he had it in his hands.

"What do you want it for? It won't do you any good. The police are on their way here now. It was Lindsey Edwards's, it wasn't yours." She screamed the words at him, half crying, half talking.

He slumped on to the floor. He was crying now and in the moment's silence that followed she was dismayed; she was shocked at his tears.

"What's the matter?" she said. It was the second time she had seen him cry.

"Lindsey Edwards was my little girl," he said, looking at her. "She was my daughter."

She was sitting in the small kitchen. The back door was open and she could see in the light the part of the garden that she and John had been in. She could see the hole and the upturned tree. He had seen them the minute he came into the kitchen. He had known all along what they were doing.

Her shoulders were slumped and her legs coiled around; her hands were loosely clasped and she wove her fingers in and out of each other.

He was making her a cup of tea. She watched him opening a small new cupboard that had appeared around a new sink unit and take out a tea caddy. The kettle had boiled and he poured some water into a china teapot. He swilled it round and tipped it into the sink.

Inside her throat her vocal cords seemed to be all tangled up. Three or four times she'd started to say something, but her tongue and her teeth got in the way. All of the things she wanted to say had "sorry" in them but every time she opened her mouth to speak the words got drowned in saliva and nothing came out.

He spooned some tea into the pot and then filled it with water. He took a tea cosy that looked like a football supporter's hat and put it over the pot.

There was silence in the room.

"Your garden's nice," she said at last, and then, shaking her head from side to side, she mocked her own stupidity. It hadn't been what she'd wanted to say.

He put a cup of tea in front of her and started to talk. It was as if he was starting a story in the middle; as if he'd already told her the first half.

"Lindy was just ten when she went missing. My wife and me – we're divorced now – we'd stopped picking her up from school, it was only two streets away, see. We were both working at the time, but usually one of us got in about fiveish. Lindy had her own key.

"She was ten. She was responsible. She usually got a drink and some biscuits and watched TV until one of us came in.

"We were living in a rented flat at the time, we'd just bought this place.

"The plans we had!" He stopped for a minute and looked around the tiny kitchen. "My wife, see, had a great sense of colour. She knew about matching wallpapers and curtains. That's where she'd been that afternoon, after work, late-night shopping, looking round furniture shops off the North Circular Road.

"I was due in at five but someone at work was having problems and I just had a quick chat. Not so quick really. I didn't get home until ten to six.

"I came through the door and called out for her, like I always did, but there was no answer. I didn't think anything of it. I went in and put the kettle on, looked in the fridge to see what we were having for tea. I called her name out again.

"There was no answer. Then I noticed the silence, not just the fact that she wasn't answering but the fact that there was no sound from the TV. I went into the bedrooms, out on to the landing. She was nowhere. I went into both neighbours but they'd not seen her. I got in the car and went round to two different pals that she had, to see if she'd gone home with them for some reason. She was nowhere. When I got back to the flat my wife was in. You know the rest. You've read it in the papers."

He stopped and Maggie took a gulp of her tea.

For the first time she thought about John Cullen. He had left her there, not knowing what might happen.

"I ought to. . ." she started to say, but he was carrying on.

"They never found her body. They still haven't found it, ten years later. In the first few weeks I kept thinking she'd turn up. I used to go to places where she and I had gone together – the Science Museum, the Zoo, Victoria Park, and I kept thinking that she might walk round the corner, or that I'd see her queuing for an ice cream or leaning against the monkey's cage. I had some idea that she might have wandered off from school by herself, that she'd lost her memory and was staying with some well-meaning person. I thought she might head for a familiar place and there I'd be. She'd slap her forehead with her hand and walk over to me and we'd just go home and everything would be like it was before.

"But they never found her body."

He stopped again. The clock on the side said twelve thirty. She wanted to go home as if this had never happened; to turn the clock back so that she could do things differently.

"My wife and me, we stayed together for a while, but things were difficult. We'd sit at the dinner table, just the two of us, and there was all this unspoken guilt. If she hadn't gone shopping, if she'd gone straight home, we could have alerted the police earlier; if I'd not stopped to talk to someone, if I'd gone home as I planned, then . . .

"My wife, my ex-wife, lives in Yorkshire now. Before she went she cleared out Lindy's things, some of them were in the box you dug up.

"It was seeing them, that was the final straw really. My

ex-wife didn't want anything you see. She wanted to forget, to make a fresh start.

"After she left I unpacked the case of stuff she'd brought and laid all the things out around me – her hair, her toys and her clothes – and I cried and cried. It was like my head was full of razor blades. They found me like that a couple of days later, the milkman it was, I think. I hadn't moved, for two days."

The air in the small kitchen was still and thick. Maggie drew breath after breath with effort. She looked around the room; the walls had been painted since she had been there. Over by the door, in a glass clipframe, was one of the photos of Lindsey Edwards. Long John looked at the picture.

"My ex-wife burned all the photos that we had. The only one I could get hold of was the one we'd given the police. I had to make do with that."

In the quiet of the night Maggie thought she heard a car pull up outside. A car door slammed.

"It's over ten years since she went missing. I always said, if they don't find her in ten years then I'll give her a decent burial."

Maggie heard her own front door slam. It would only be minutes now before her dad realized she wasn't there.

"I decided on a magnolia tree. I know it's not the best time to plant them, but it was well established. I thought it would take."

There was a knock at the door. Maggie didn't know whether to get up or not. Long John didn't seem to hear it.

She began to rise from her chair. He leant over suddenly and held her hand on the table with his.

"I still miss her, even now."

He lifted his hand and sat back. A more impatient knock sounded. Maggie ran along the hall, her feet like lead.

Her dad was there, his face a mixture of smiles and alarm.

"Where have you been? I was just about to phone the police."

"I was a bit scared on my own. . ." She was going to say that she'd come next door for company with Mr Young, but he spoke over the top of her words.

"Your mum's done it!" he said. He seemed to be jumping from one foot to the other. "Thanks, Eddie," he shouted into the house. Long John was walking along the hall towards them. Maggie took her dad's hand to lead him away. His joy was completely out of place.

"Eleven and a half hours in labour. I thought it would never happen."

"How did it go?" Long John had walked up the hall.

"Come on, Dad." Maggie was pulling him along the path. She didn't want him to blurt out the news just then.

"Don't you want to hear?" he said, looking delightedly at them both.

Maggie's shoulders dropped.

"It's a girl," he said. "A lovely baby girl! Seven pounds two ounces.

Long John's mouth curved into a slow smile.

"Brilliant," he said. "Give my best to your wife." Behind the smile his eyes were dull. Her dad didn't notice, though, and slapped him roundly on the shoulder, as if they were long-time friends. He closed the door gently as Maggie listened to her dad chattering as they went along the path and into their own house.

TWENTY

Babies are funny things, Maggie thought as she sat watching her sister through the bars of the cot.

She was pale and wrinkled and there were scaly bits of skin around her hairline as though she had dandruff and didn't use the right shampoo. It was hot outside but her mum had still dressed her in a babygro; she was covered in fabric from her neck to her toes. Her tiny red hands poked out of the sleeves, the fingers making small fists, as though she were ready for a fight.

Her eyes were closed, though, and she was sound asleep. That was mostly all she'd done for the past five days: sleep and feed; sleep and feed.

For once she was lying in relative solitude; no mum or dad or relatives or neighbours peering down at her. Only Maggie was there, a list of instructions inside her head about "How To Look After a Newborn Baby". On the chest of drawers was an opened packet of disposable nappies (as though Maggie wasn't capable of opening a packet); a tiny bottle with an ounce or so of milk that had been expressed from her mother's breast; a box of baby wipes; the phone number of the doctor.

Her mother had gone shopping to Mothercare to buy some new bras. Nothing fitted any more. The lump had more or less gone but now her breasts had enlarged and looked like two quivering balloons. Now and then Maggie's eyes were drawn by damp patches slowly forming near the centre of each breast. It was the milk, she knew, although she'd never thought it would just turn itself on and off like that.

Her mum had metamorphosed; she had turned into a large, soft machine that provided for The Baby. Her breasts were its food, her knees and shoulders were rests that the baby lay over; her hands patted and rubbed the baby's back until it emitted exclamations of wind that filled the room and brought a gasp or a smile to her parents' lips.

Now and then her dad offered his bony knees or his clumsy hands to lift or cradle her. She wasn't happy, though; her face crumpled and reddened and she cried, as though someone had just told her she was about to be tortured. Give us here, give us here, her mum would say and her dad, defeated, would hand over the infant and retreat into the front room with his newspaper.

They were going to call her Sarah.

Maggie looked down at her. She tried to imagine herself saying to Bridget, "This is my sister, Sarah," or "My sister Sarah said" or "My little sister, Sarah. . ."

In a few days Bridget would be back from Ireland. Then she would tell her all the things that had happened.

Maggie walked over to the window and looked into the gardens. She'd been told to stay in the baby's room. Keep listening to her breathing, her mum had insisted; don't leave the room, don't let the cover go over her head, careful that she doesn't bring up her last feed; make sure she's lying on her side.

Long John was in his garden. He had a pair of jeans on but no top. He was raking dry grass from the yellowing lawn. Over to his right was the magnolia tree, replanted. On one of the thin twigs Maggie could see something hanging loosely. It was a ribbon.

She thought of John Cullen heaving the tree out of the ground, of the terrified expression on his face before he ran away. She'd not seen him since that night. She had no wish to see him again; not after he'd left her there.

Long John had been in his front garden when her mum was getting out of the car with the new baby. He'd looked at the baby and smiled. He'd made clicking noises in the back of his throat and asked about its weight, its length.

Maggie had noticed that his hair had been washed and he'd looked alert.

Maggie hadn't joined in the pleasantries. She'd looked into Long John's eyes, along the downward curve of his eyebrow, and into the lines that hung down from the side of his mouth. She'd looked at him with apprehension and for a moment, as they'd walked away from him, up the path, her mum carrying the baby, her dad a giant packet of disposable nappies, she'd wanted to touch him or squeeze his hand. He'd turned quickly away though and she'd felt the vibrations as his front door slammed shut.

She didn't see him again for four days. There'd been no sounds from his house and at night she'd looked out of her bedroom window to see if he was anywhere about.

His light shone into the back garden as usual but she never saw him wander out. She'd heard the baby crying early in the morning and got up and gone into her parents' room where the baby lay alongside her mum sucking noisily at her nipple. She'd wandered around chatting vacantly about this and that and from time to time looked out of the bay window in case he was going out somewhere early.

Was he all right?

Once or twice she'd sat and imagined the worst.

Long John, she must stop calling him that, Eddie, was unstable (who wouldn't be after what had happened). He'd been let out of hospital and had resettled in his old area using a different name. He had been trying to make a fresh start, then a local girl went missing, just as his own daughter had ten years before. The same man was picked up for questioning who had been taken into custody in connection with his daughter's disappearance.

Instead of getting over it, making a fresh start, "Long John" Eddie had moved right back into the middle of it all. On top of that there was his next-door neighbour's daughter and her friends who suspected him of being the abductor. They teased him, they watched him. Two of them broke into his back garden and stole his daughter's belongings from the grave he had just put them into.

At the very same time there was a new baby girl next door. Small and pink and smelling of milk and talcum powder.

Had it reminded him of his own daughter?

Had he gone back into his own house and thought about suicide? Maggie held a great bubble of fear in her stomach that he would do something to himself. From time to time she hovered by his gate daring herself to go up and knock. But what could she say?

On the fourth day, after her mum and dad's car pulled away from the pavement, his door suddenly opened and he came out. He was dressed in a suit. His hair was short. He looked altogether different. She'd watched him from her window as he got into his car and drove off.

He was all right then; a heavy weight had lifted off her shoulders.

From the spare-room window she watched him as he sat down in one of the old deckchairs and lit a cigarette. He looked up at her. Her instinct was to pull back to hide behind the curtain but she couldn't do it.

She raised her hand and waved.

He nodded his head at her and his eyes left her and swung slowly round the garden. He looked much younger with his hair cut.

What would Amy say when she told her the full details? They had had the wrong man. She had picked on the wrong man.

She sat down in the chair that her mother used for breastfeeding.

It was the second time in her life that the wrong man had been picked on because of her.

It was the second time.

* * *

"It's like this, sir," the policeman said to her mum and dad, "Mr Cotton doesn't deny that your daughter came into his shop. He doesn't deny that he chatted to her or that she sat on his knee." The policeman paused to take a mouthful of tea. "He does, however, deny that he touched your daughter in any inappropriate way. It's his view that she asked him to tell her a story and that she sat on his knee. He says it would have seemed unfriendly to tell her to get off. He says his own children sit on his knee to listen to stories."

Maggie heard very little of this. What she had focused on was that the Material Man's name was Mr Cotton. Cotton! He was the Complete Material Man. For a few seconds, while the policeman's voice droned on, she imagined him unbuttoning his waistcoat and shirt and underneath, instead of skin, there was the colourless fabric that the bodies of rag dolls were made of. Even though she knew it couldn't be true, he was frozen in her mind like a great floppy doll. Mr Cotton.

"You see, sir, don't think for a minute that we don't believe your daughter. No, no. She told her story to three different officers. We also have the version she told to her friend. Each time all the facts are consistent. No, no. We believe your daughter was sexually assaulted. We believe Mr Cotton was the man who did it.

"The question is, what do we do about it? Your daughter will only have one chance on the witness stand. The prosecution will ask her to tell her story. She will tell it, truthfully, as she has told us. The defence will cross-examine her testimony, aggressively, to say the least. They will question her over and over about whether she could have been mistaken. They will go over detail after detail, trying to trip her. They will say she could have been fanciful and exaggerated what happened. If they fail to move her they will say she concocted it with a friend. In the end, if they don't rattle her they will call her a liar. The question is, sir, with no guarantee of convicting this man, do you want to put your daughter through that? May I?" The policeman pointed to a plate of sandwiches that had appeared on the coffee table.

Maggie thought of herself peeping up from behind a wooden stand; to her right an old man in a white wig. Men in long black coats all around her. Across the room, inside a fenced-off area, Mr Cotton, the Material Man.

The policeman had stopped talking and was taking giant bites of the sandwiches her mum had provided. Maggie could hear her dad's voice getting louder, her mum's accompanying "Shh . . . shh. . ."

And inside the Material Man were wire ribs and sponge lungs. Instead of veins and arteries there were long pieces of thick red and blue embroidery thread that led to a red velvet heart.

Her dad's voice was getting louder in her head. The policeman had stopped eating sandwiches and was standing up. Her dad was standing up. Her dad was swearing, calling Mr Cotton dreadful names, using words that she had been told never to use.

She imagined Mr Cotton cheek's reddening at what was

being said about him. That was impossible. He had no feelings. He was made of sponge with a velvet heart.

She shouldn't have sat on his knee. Maybe it was her fault.

Her mum was crying and had her hand on her dad's shoulder. The policeman was taking his notebook out. He had a quick look at it and then folded it up and put it back into his pocket.

Maybe it was all her fault.

She started to cry.

Her dad stopped his shouting and her mum looked across at her. The policeman sat down again.

Her dad came over and hugged her. She could feel his arms shaking.

The policeman started to speak again.

"You see, sir, in cases like this, we believe that the best thing to do is to put the whole complaint on file. That means that your daughter's statement is on our files indefinitely. The next time there's a complaint in the area against any young girl, whoever she is, wherever it happens, we'll bring Cotton into the station as a possible suspect. He'll be questioned, he may have to go into an identity parade. His family will be questioned. In short, sir, from now on this man will have to answer for his movements whenever a young girl is assaulted in this way."

There was silence.

"You mark my words, sir, it will not be a pleasant experience for the man. It's not prison, I'll grant you that, but it's not freedom either. And one day –" the policeman took the last sandwich – "one day he'll slip up. One day there'll be more evidence than just one little girl. And then we'll get him."

Maggie watched from her parents' bedroom window as the policeman walked off down the street. Her mum and dad came into the room.

"Maggie," her dad said, "you heard it all. It's what we think is for the best. There's just one thing left to do. Tomorrow I'm going to go over to Cotton's shop and just tell him what I think of him. And then it'll all be over and we can continue as if nothing ever happened. Do you understand?"

Maggie nodded her head.

"It's something I have to do. I have to see the man. I have to let him see me. I want him to know that little girls like you aren't on their own. Do you see?"

Maggie nodded but she didn't really see. Her mum sat beside her and gave her a hug.

"We'll have a good holiday this year. We need it!" Her dad said it lightly but she knew that his words were false, that he was tense.

The next day she watched him at breakfast. He ate each spoonful of his cereal with determination and sat tapping his fingers on the table after he'd turned each page of his newspaper. At nine thirty he got up and left. She looked at her mum for some reassurance but she was staring into the garden.

Would he be violent? Would he grab the Material Man

by his glittering waistcoat and throw him about the shop? Like they did in films?

Would he, quite literally, "knock the stuffing" out of the little, breathless man, leaving nothing but remnants of fabric floating in the heavy atmosphere of the shop?

What would he do?

She went up to her bedroom and waited.

She could hear her mum rattling knives and forks in the kitchen downstairs.

About an hour later the front door opened. Maggie held her breath with anticipation.

She sat still for a few minutes waiting to be called. She began to hear a strange noise that she couldn't put a name to. It was rhythmic and throaty. She was afraid. What had happened? Why didn't they call her?

She heard it again, louder and louder. Then she heard her mum's voice joining in, making the same noise.

It was laughter.

They were laughing about something.

She ran downstairs and flung open the kitchen door. Her mum was bent over the sink, her hand on her chest, shaking with uncontrollable laughs. Her dad was sitting back on one of the chairs, his leg rising and falling with each loud guffaw.

Maggie sat on the floor, her legs bent up, her arms around them, her chin on her knees and watched them until she too, without knowing why, began to smile, just a little at first and then, without any warning, the laughter burst out of her throat and joined the rest that was dancing around the room.

Her mum told the story better than her dad. Three or four times that day Maggie wanted to hear it, over and over.

"Your dad went over to Middle Lane. I told him where it was. I said to him, 'It's the material shop in Middle Lane.' I didn't think, see. There's another material shop, on the corner, next to the motorbike place. I never go there, it's too expensive. It's owned by Mr and Mrs McCarthy. You know her – her daughter's in the next class up from you. She's always in the best of gear. Anyway, your dad only goes in there. He only goes in the wrong shop.

"I wouldn't mind but he looks around for a while. There's Mr McCarthy laying out bales of fabric, and your dad just waits. He wants an audience see; it's no good going to shame the man if there's no one to see it.

"Eventually a couple of old women come in. He walks to the counter. 'I want to speak to you,' he says to McCarthy. Apparently his wife has appeared at this time too. He looks around and waits until these two old dears are watching as well. 'Are you the man who molested my daughter?' he says, and everyone stops talking and stares at your dad. 'Are you? Are you the sort of man who interferes with young girls?'

"Mr McCarthy turns red and his wife comes over. Your dad looks round. 'This man molested my daughter a few days ago. Come on, Cotton, admit it now!'

"Mrs McCarthy's mouth drops open. Mr McCarthy is frozen to the spot. The old dears start to speak. 'Did you say Mr Cotton? Mr Cotton owns the other material shop, up the street on the other side. Mr Cotton owns that shop. Not this. This is Mr McCarthy.'

"'This is Mr McCarthy,' Mrs McCarthy says. Everyone is pointing at Mr McCarthy.

"It was your dad's mouth that fell open then. He said that a tube train could have come out of it. He just looked around at all these people and realized what a mistake he'd made. He just sat down then on the floor and leant his back against the counter and started to cry.

"Mr and Mrs McCarthy were very nice about it, he said.

They made him a cup of tea and got him a chair. The two old ladies got out their hankies and forced him to take them. The more desperate he got, the happier and more chirpy the McCarthys got. He says he told them the whole story. The old ladies sat up on the counter, he said, so that they could hear it all.

"Eventually he got away and walked across the road towards Cotton's shop. When he looked back they were all standing outside the McCarthys', watching him. When he got there it was closed. 'On holiday for two weeks', the sign said.

"It was when your dad was walking back and he passed by the McCarthys' that he began to see the funny side of it. They waved to him and they had a shop full of people. He was sure that they were telling the whole story and spreading the dirt about Mr Cotton."

After the story her mum made a cup of tea. A week later they went on holiday to Torquay.

It had been funny, that time, when they'd got the wrong man. They'd all laughed.

Maggie took another look at Long John (Eddie) in his deckchair. No one was laughing this time.

TWENTY-ONE

Maggie posted her letter to Bridget with all the baby's details. It would be the last letter. She was due back at the weekend. It had been a long six weeks.

She walked past the flats and wondered about Caroline Mitchell and the man the police had had in for questioning. The local paper she had read said that they had released him without charge. It was history repeating itself; Caroline would probably never be seen again, her disappearance a mystery to the police.

Walking across the road, she heard her name being called from the other direction.

She knew it was Amy back from her holiday. She quickened her pace, pretending that she hadn't heard. She did not want to have a conversation with Amy. More than anything else, it meant filling her in on all that had happened since she went away. It meant telling her all the mistakes they – she – had made.

"Maggie," Amy's voice had a shrill ring to it. Maggie didn't look round but opened her gate and went in.

At the same time she didn't want to see John Cullen. Since he had deserted her in Long John's garden she could no longer pretend any romantic involvement with him. The fact that he had run off and left her to an unknown fate meant that she could hardly use him as part of any story to tell Bridget when she got back.

If she got into conversation with Amy it was likely that he would breeze up and, out of politeness, she would have to talk to him.

She just got her key in the lock when Amy puffed up behind her. She couldn't ignore her now.

"Maggie, something's happened. John's. . ." Amy took deep breaths between each word. Perhaps if she didn't smoke so much, Maggie thought.

"John's gone. John's gone missing," Amy finally said.

"Missing?" Maggie said. "What do you mean?" Maggie couldn't help but roll her eyes.

"We got back from holiday today and he's not been home for days. None of the letters have been picked up off the mat. The woman next door says she's not seen him since last Friday. I went down to his stall in the market and he's not been there either. I don't know what's happened."

"Has your mum contacted the police?"

"No. She just thinks he's gone off with his mates. She says not to worry, but I am worried."

Maggie looked at Amy, whose face was beginning to redden.

"But what makes you think he hasn't just gone off with his mates?"

"Because he doesn't have any mates. Why do you think he hangs round with me?"

"But what about his football-training mates."

"He doesn't go football training."

"Still. . ." Maggie looked at her watch. Why should she care what had happened to John Cullen? "He's probably gone off to visit his dad on the oil rigs. Why don't you ring up your dad and see if he's there?" she added with sarcasm in her voice.

"Maggie, please. You don't understand. There's things you don't know." Amy was crying and she'd grabbed Maggie's arm. "I know something's wrong. I found this in his bed."

Amy held out a girl's T-shirt. It was orange and grubby. It had a tear in the side.

"What is it?"

"It's Caroline's," she said. "It belonged to Caroline Mitchell."

It was nine o'clock and Amy and Maggie were sitting side by side on top of the signal box in Lousy Park.

Amy had been crying but had stopped; she was holding one of Maggie's hands. On her lap was a small grubby stuffed monkey with a plastic dummy in its mouth that Maggie had never seen before.

"Me and John used to come here late at night. To get away from me dad."

Maggie didn't answer. She was looking across the deserted buildings to the lights of the homes and shops where ordinary people lived and thinking about the awful story that Amy had just told her.

"How long has he been in prison?" she finally said.

"Two years. That's when the council moved us. Two years ago."

"Do you ever see him?" Maggie tried to visualize a man to fit an image of Amy and John's dad. The picture came up with someone seedy and breathless, a man in small gold glasses who pretended to be kind to children.

"Don't want to see him. Neither does John."

Maggie held Amy's hand tighter. In the distance she could hear a faint police siren and the sounds of the engines of cars or buses. People were getting on and off buses, unaware of the story that Amy had told her. Families in cars were going to visit friends, unaware of what she had just heard. In shops all over the area people were buying sweets or cigarettes or wine; they didn't know that Amy and John Cullen's dad was in prison because he had done bad things to them.

How could people carry on as normal when there were such ugly things going on in the dark of a child's bedroom?

Had there been toys around? Had they been thrown out of the way, shoved under the bed? She pictured them in some sort of untidy pile, a doll or Action Man on top, lying askew, the eyes closed; just a sad plastic face that could see or hear nothing.

Maggie's thoughts were interrupted by another police siren, this time closer to where they were sitting.

"I wish I knew where John was," Amy said, her voice plaintive against the growing siren, now doubled with another and a few seconds later a couple more.

No wonder John and Amy were a bit strange. Amy the sophisticate and John the overgrown kid. Except for the kissing. He knew how to do that.

"Something big's happened," Amy said, straining her eyes into the distance. The lights were moving towards them.

"They're coming down on to the estate," Maggie said. "Let's go and see." She began to climb down the side of the signal box. Amy stayed where she was.

"Are you coming?"

"I just wish I knew where John was," she said, turning herself round so that she could climb down.

Maggie took Amy's hand again and led her through the alleys between the disused buildings. In the distance she could hear the sounds of car engines and in the dark sky she could see the light given off by their headlights.

"What I don't understand," Maggie said in a loud whisper, "is how come your mum didn't know about it. Why didn't your mum stop him coming into your bedroom?"

"Ssh. . ." Amy had stopped. She wasn't listening to her. Maggie could hear voices up ahead and the crackles of radio receivers in the cars. Up the hill she could still see the blue lights swinging round and in the distance could hear yet another siren, far away at first and then getting closer.

They came to an opening in the outbuildings of the old factory. There, in what used to be the car park, were the police cars. There were two policemen standing leaning against the bonnet of one. The others had gone somewhere. They were joined by a fourth car whose siren had been silenced but which came to a screeching halt on the cracked-up surface, sending a shower of small stones into the air. The doors were open almost before the car had stopped and two policemen rushed out. Maggie could hear one of the others shout, "Behind the main building," and the newly arrived officers ran off in that direction.

Maggie and Amy crouched down in the shadows, Amy holding her toy monkey close to her face.

When Amy had told her story Maggie's face had had a look of shock and amazement. After a couple of minutes, when it had sunk in, she'd adopted her usual expression of cynical disbelief. She had been waiting for Amy to start shrieking and saying, "You believed me! "

But she hadn't; she'd just held on to her toy monkey and cried.

"What's happening?" Maggie said, her eyes on the police cars in the distance. One of the police who had gone off to the buildings was returning. He was shouting something to the others.

Why had their mother not put a stop to it? She looked at Amy's profile. She must have been seven or eight when it was happening. Then there was John, why had he not told someone? She glanced back towards the police cars where something seemed to be happening. A van had arrived and a couple of men were getting shovels and tools out from the back of it.

And why had John run away?

"My mum made me and John swear never to tell anybody. I only told Caroline. She was my best friend."

"Caroline Mitchell knew?" Maggie remembered Caroline's face, with its mean grin. "She wasn't the best person to tell," she said, but Amy wasn't looking at her any more. Amy's gaze had been drawn away by the scene in front of the factories and she began to walk out of their hiding place towards the police cars.

"Stop. . ." Maggie started to say, but then she looked at the policemen coming from the far buildings. Between them was a third figure, walking unsteadily. It was too dark to make out the features but Maggie knew who it was. She knew why Amy was running towards him.

After a few seconds the two policemen got back to the cars. John Cullen stood between them, his hands shielding his eyes from the harsh lights.

Amy ran into the middle of them, past the policeman who was standing watch and in between the two that flanked her brother. She put her arms round him.

"What's going on!"

"Oi!"

'You can't come here!" the policemen shouted out

Maggie walked towards the group, a terrible foreboding taking hold of her. As she placed one foot in front of the other, unconnected things kept springing into her head.

"Oi, there's another kid over there," she heard a policeman yell.

John Cullen had been the last person to see Caroline alive, he said. He saw her get into the back of a black car.

He was on his way to football training.

More cars were arriving. A small black van, like the one she'd seen up at the ponds that day when the frogmen were there.

John Cullen didn't go to football training. He had no mates. He hung around with his sister. Before her friend disappeared he hung around with both of them.

Maggie's steps were leading her towards the centre. There was John, standing in the dark, looking afraid. It was the way she had last seen him in Long John's garden just before he had run away, leaving her to face him alone.

Had he come straight here?

None of the police seemed to be taking much notice of her. A stretcher came out of the black van and a plain black car pulled up among the throng.

"That the pathologist?" she heard someone shout above the cacophony.

"The body's this way." Another voice distinguishable from the rest.

"Over by the back buildings. Under the flooring."

"A small shed. There's officers there."

"Got the lights set up?"

Maggie reached John and Amy. He was standing between two policeman, she was holding his arm. She looked young now. Her brother, his face gaunt and frightened, looked old.

Maggie looked over towards the back buildings. There was a small crowd of people there; a portable floodlight had been set up and there were wires along the ground.

The buzz of a dozen conversations was broken occasionally by the sound of interference on someone's radio.

Over there was Caroline's body. Only feet away from where they'd been messing about a few weeks ago.

All the time she'd been lying there, night and day, for six weeks.

Maggie turned her head away and there on the floor was the toy monkey. Amy had dropped it in her hurry to get to her brother. She picked it up and held on to it tightly.

TWENTY-TWO

The removals van was almost ready to go. Maggie watched as the driver tipped up a bottle of Coke and drank from it. The sound of the van's radio spilt into the street. Amy was sitting on the wall beside her, tapping her foot to the sound of a hit song.

"Where will you go to school?" Maggie said.

"Dunno." Amy was holding her toy monkey, taking the dummy out of its mouth and putting it back. On the wall beside her was a packet of cigarettes that she had just taken out of her pocket.

"Why don't you give them up?" Maggie said.

"When I start me new school," she said, moving the monkey's arms around, "then I'll give up."

"Aymmmeeeee!" Maggie heard the shout from far inside the flats. Amy put the cigarettes back inside her pocket and standing up, said, "They're good trainers," and walked away.

Maggie looked down at her new trainers. She'd bought them with the accumulated pound coins that her dad had given her over the summer. Her dad had added another ten-pound note to her savings when the police had brought her home from Lousy Park the night John got arrested.

Her dad had gone to the police station with Amy's mum

to find out what was happening to John. He had come home looking grim; Amy's mum and Amy had gone to stay with relatives.

John Cullen had written a letter to the police himself. In it he'd told them he'd killed Caroline. He'd told them where to find him. And where to find her body.

Someone said he'd posted the letter; someone else said he'd given it to a friend to give in at the police station. (Maggie knew that wasn't true. Apart from her and Amy, he had no friends.)

The police had ignored it at first, thinking it was just a hoax like all the others.

Then there'd been a phone call from John's mum after she'd gone into his room and found other things of Caroline's, her purse, her other trainer, her rings.

Nobody knew exactly what had happened. Maggie had not been able to think about it without feeling panic and shame. She had been alone with John over and over again. She had let him kiss her and touch her.

John Cullen was a sick boy, her dad had said. He won't be sent to prison, he'll be sent to a psychiatric hospital.

Now the family was being moved, "for their own protection". Amy and her mum starting somewhere fresh like they did two years ago.

The driver of the removals van beeped a signal for Amy and her mum to hurry up. Maggie looked at her watch. Bridget's plane would be taking off about now. In a few hours she'd be back. Maggie felt a buzz of anticipation in her chest.

"We're off then," Amy said, walking out of the flats towards her. She was followed by her mum, whose shoulders were rounded and whose eyes darted in all directions as she walked from the flats to the van. Maggie looked around. Apart from Mrs Rogers cleaning the brick wall outside her house she could see no one else.

"Look after yourself," Maggie called as Amy squeezed into the front of the van beside her mother and the driver.

As Maggie turned to walk home she noticed a man outside number fifty putting a "For Sale" sign into the front garden. She ignored Mrs Rogers, who looked as though she was ready for a chat, and went straight indoors and into the kitchen.

"Mr Young's leaving, then?" she said.

"Yes, he wants to make a fresh start. He says there are too many memories in this area for him. I wonder where he'll go?" Her mum was changing the baby's nappy and Maggie was faced with a pool of what looked like light brown poster paint. She glanced out of the back garden window.

She wondered how much her mother knew about Long John. Did she know about his daughter? A couple of times, since she had come home from hospital, Maggie had wanted to tell her. She'd even started talking generally about Long John, intending to drop into the conversation the things she had learned about him.

The trouble was it meant explaining how she knew these things. It involved telling about the things she had done and the mistakes she had made.

She decided to keep it to herself. Her mum was always pleased to drop the conversation anyway and start to talk about the baby.

"Here, put this in the bin, will you, love." She handed Maggie the soiled nappy and picked the baby up off the table.

Maggie held the nappy at arm's length and, opening the kitchen bin with her foot, dropped it in.

"It's sad about him. He found it hard to get on with people," her mum said. "He was better with plants, though. His garden is beautiful. That magnolia tree will be gorgeous in a couple of years."

Bridget was on her way round. She'd phoned Maggie the minute she'd got home from the airport and now it was only five or ten minutes until she would see her again.

Bridget said she had a lot to tell her and then there'd been a suggestive laugh over the phone which implied that there were a great many salacious details to be revealed.

She'd smiled but her heart wasn't in it. She'd said that she had a lot to tell Bridget but she knew she wouldn't. How could she put it all into words? Caroline Mitchell was dead; John was in custody; Amy and her mum had gone to some other part of the borough where nobody knew about them; Long John had left.

Maggie pictured him walking down his pathway, his battered suitcase in one hand and his black plastic bin liner over his shoulder. Had she been the cause of his going away? Had it been her fault?

The questions hung in the air around her and she couldn't answer them.

She heard the doorbell ring and the baby cry together; a second or so later two voices, her mum and her dad, from different parts of the house, shouted, "I'll get it!"

She knew that they were both rushing towards whichever room the baby was in.

Walking down the stairs, towards Bridget's shadow on the front door, she smiled.

Sarah. It was a pretty nice name, all in all.

also by anne cassidy

The Story of my

LIFE

The last thing Kenny Harris wanted was blood on his hands. He almost smiled at this thought. Wasn't it too late to worry about such things? He was in too deep. He couldn't turn back now.

He was standing on Leyton platform. The Central Line. Not a place he usually went to. Above him a clock hung like a huge blank face, its hands stuck at three-forty. He looked at his mobile to check the time. 22:48. He thought of Nat waiting for him at her house. He imagined himself trying to explain it all to her. The mess he was in. He found the words of an argument playing through his mind. He saw himself appealing to her. *I wasn't always like this*, he would say, his hands out in supplication.

He had to stop. The air was heavy with rain but there wasn't a sound as it hit the ground. The clock stared sullenly and he took a deep breath. He looked down at his bruised hand, his battered jeans, his busted-up trainers. With his good hand he felt above his eyebrow for the cut. It had stopped bleeding but was swollen and sore to touch.

He shivered with the cold. He turned and looked along the track for the glow of an approaching train but there was just a thick slice of blackness. He listened intently for a second. There it was, he was sure, in the distance; the rhythmic clatter of the wheels.

Where are you, Tommy?

The words ran through his head. A couple of people appeared on the platform opposite. A man and a woman, standing silently side by side. Like two ghosts that had come from nowhere.

Tommy Fortune. Where are you?

The man opposite said something to the woman. She turned her head away. In the distance there was the sound of a car braking. A sudden screech that set Kenny's teeth on edge.

He had five, six hours left to find him.

The drizzle turned to rain abruptly. Just like that. It hammered on to the tracks and Kenny stepped back, away from the platform edge, into the dry. He watched the rain spearing down, invisible in the darkness but under the light it shone like steel.

His hand touched the back pocket of his jeans. The letter was there, folded in two. He'd taken days to write it and now it was finished. What would he do with it?

Something fluttered in his stomach. He could walk away. Leave things to sort themselves out. But wouldn't that just make Mack more angry? And make things worse?

His hands were cold. He shoved them into his jacket pocket and grimaced as pain shot through his injured fingers. It made him feel nauseous for a moment. No, worse than that. The shock of the beating came back to him. Being thrown around like a rag doll. His fingers held in a vice-like grip; a punch to the head, a kick in the thigh. From the ground he'd looked up expecting more but there was just the sound of the car pulling away, revving up the road leaving him like a rubbish bag on the street.

Was he afraid of Mack? Yes he was. After tonight, Tommy Fortune would be afraid of him as well.

He steeled himself. *Keep calm.* With his good hand he cradled his bruised fingers, his crushed knuckle. If he could just get *warm*.

Looking along the track he saw the distant light of the train. He'd been right, had heard it from miles away. One stop to Stratford and then he would get the Docklands Light Railway to Poplar. It wouldn't take him long. He breathed deeply but felt his chest tightening. He coughed a couple of times and searched around in his pockets for his inhaler. He shook it and frowned. It felt empty. Pretty soon he wouldn't be able to breathe at all. He'd have no choice but to go home. He put it in his mouth and inhaled gently as the train rumbled in filling the platform with yellow light.

He got into the carriage and sat in the first seat available, his legs splayed. It was almost empty. Just one old bald man sitting in the corner seat a book open on his lap. He looked over at Kenny his forehead wrinkling. Kenny turned away. Exactly how bad did he look? The man went back at his book, crossing his legs as if to ward Kenny off.

Kenny made himself focus on the window. They were still above ground. The rain was hitting the glass in darts and he leaned back, feeling the warmth of the carriage, and closed his eyes. After a while he felt the suck of the train as it went back underground.

He got off at Stratford. Like Leyton, the station was above ground and even though it was late the platform was busy. People were standing in groups waiting for over-ground trains or walking towards the exits to change on to other lines. The platforms were brightly lit up, bathed in the lights from the nearby high-rise buildings. Kenny squinted into the light. He saw the rain turning into snow before his eyes. In the windows of the glass buildings he could see triangles of coloured lights on Christmas trees. It was all too bright, too cheerful. He turned away and walked briskly towards the darker end of the station where the Docklands Light Railway terminated.

There was one other person standing waiting. A young woman with a baby in a pushchair. When he got closer he could see that she was younger than he'd thought. Fourteen, fifteen maybe. She had hardly any hair and a piercing right in the middle of her top lip. The baby, a toddler, was sound asleep. She gave him a funny look and started to back away, reversing the pushchair. He backed off himself. He must look a fright.

A beeping sound made him turn away. He pulled his mobile out and looked at the screen. Two messages. His fingers were too sore and stiff to press the buttons so he had to use his other hand. It took a minute.

The first message was from Nat. *Where are you? I've waited all night!!!*

The second was from Mack. *Don't forget. By six at the latest. Bring Tommy to the Sugar House.*

He had to find him first.

From out of the dark he saw a square of light. It was small and bright and he could hear the sound of it chugging towards him. The DLR. The train that didn't need a driver. He watched it get bigger and finally trundle into the station. The first time he had travelled on it he had been thrilled. He'd sat at the front as though he, himself, was the driver. How old had he been? Eight, nine? Just a boy.

The doors opened and half a dozen people got off. The woman with the pushchair walked towards the front end and got on. Kenny went to the rear carriage and sat down. He snapped his mobile shut. It lay in his good hand cold and solid. It was brand new, his birthday present from his mum and dad. His birthday, ten days before. A day he wanted to forget. He squeezed his eyelids shut. He would push it away. He would close it up behind some heavy door in his head. His seventeenth birthday. The worst night of his life.

He stared at his reflection in the glass opposite. Ghostly. Ghastly.

The doors of the train closed and a second later it moved off, into the darkness.